Warehouse of the Dead

A Novela

Holding the Line

Memorable Calls

Autobiographical

Warehouse of the Dead

Holding the Line

Memorable Calls

Michael Cunningham

Washington, USA

Cover photo by Pixabay/pixels.com
Cover design by Michael Cunningham
mikecunningham@gmail.com

ISBN 978-0-578-72031-9

Printed in the United States of America

"God, help my head to forget what my eyes have seen, and my heart has endured."
—Thomas Cheshire

Reviews

This is a fast paced action novella followed by 21 chapters of biographical events.

The novella tells the story of a broken and flawed fire inspector trying to discover who burned down a nondescript factory building filled with cadavers. There is a gritty and realistic feel to the characters and settings. This novella ends all too soon, and I hope the author writes more about this or other characters.

The biographic chapters describe what urban firefighting is really like, with all its tragedy, comedy, pathos, and absurdity. … If Hollywood wants to get firefighting right they need to do a comedy. Chapter 37 of this book ("It Only Hurts When I Laugh") is a good place to start. *K. Barry* ★★★★★

I worked many years with the author. He knows his subject. The first part of the book is a fictional story that is similar to a real case the author investigated. It kept my interest and I quickly went through it.

The last parts of the book are biographical and listed a number of actual events the author was involved with. I think I enjoyed these parts of the books more than the fictional part. I found out more about the author than I had known previously and his reviewing past incidents, some I was directly involved in, was quite interesting. It took me back to my own past.

I recommend "Warehouse Of The Dead!"

M. Reardon ★★★★★

Love this novella as it was a quick read with short chapters. The story line had some very unexpected turns that caught me off guard. It definitely ended too soon. I wanted more. Since this is the first book that I picked up in about three years and finished, I'm happy that the story kept my attention. *Karen A* ★★★★★

Dedication

To my loving wife Debbie, sons, James and Jared, and to the many firefighters, peace officers, attorneys, agents, partners and insurance adjusters I have worked with and alongside. I thank you. Without your support, patience and understanding, my career, of over 30 years, would not have been as enjoyable.

Thanks also to God, whose hand must have been on my shoulder, from my early days; leading me to, and through, a career in which I responded to over 30,000 emergency calls, and hundreds of investigations over the span of more than 30 years.

Thanks also to my daughter-in-laws, Nicole and Crystal, for their literary help. A special thanks to my brother, Dave, for his literary help and for suggesting I become a firefighter. Thanks also to Gerald Moriarty for the inspiration to get this book out of my head and on to paper.

About the Author

Michael Cunningham is the eldest son of an aerospace engineer and an aspiring actress mother. He has two brothers and a sister. They spent their formative years in the Rolling Hills Estates portion of what is known as the Palos Verdes Peninsula. Michael was active in youth groups and sports growing up.

His intentions were to be an illustrator, and he was going to school to learn the trade when he was drafted into the Army. After his Army duty ended, Michael returned to school, intent on becoming a teacher. Frustration and illness eventually led him to focus on a career in firefighting.

He became proficient in fire investigations and eventually obtained a private investigators license, working a second job investigating fires for insurance companies for over 15 years.

Michael suffered injuries when he and his crew fell through the roof of a burning building. Politics and high blood pressure almost ended his career when he began suffering panic attacks at age 50. That challenge conquered, Michael went on to spend five more years fighting fires and an additional 10 years investigating them.

Contents

PART II   Holding the Line

PART III   Memorable Calls

Part I

Warehouse of the Dead

Portions of this story are loosely based on actual events and persons, but characters and events have been blended and fictionalized. None of the characters are intended to represent any real person, living or dead.

Chapter I

Wake-up Call

Thomas Cheshire was off duty and had taken an Oxycodone, as he had done each night for over a year, just to sleep. He went through the same silent prayer every night: "God, help my head to forget what my eyes have seen and my heart has endured." He wasn't the first and wouldn't be the last firefighter to feel that way. He just couldn't get past that horrible day 13 months prior.

Thomas' sleep was broken by phone call at 1:30 a.m. That in itself was not unusual for an arson investigator. Thomas was accustomed to being awakened from a dead sleep by a ring. But this time, the case would haunt him for a very long time.

"Investigator Cheshire, this is dispatch," the voice said. "Your Battalion Chief has asked you to respond to 23802 Canyon Road for an investigation."

"Um ... yeah, I can be there in 45 minutes to an hour."

Rubbing the sleep from his eyes, Thomas dressed in his uniform quickly. He grabbed the bag with overalls, a flashlight, small hand tools and a clipboard. Thomas strapped his 9mm Smith and Wesson to his hip and slung his 35mm camera over his shoulder before he headed out the door.

He jumped into the Chevy truck he had bought more than a decade earlier, when he was setting off on a much different profession. Buying the new Silverado truck was his first order of business after Thomas signed his big baseball contract. Thomas and his high school girlfriend, Amber, had gone down to the dealership and paid cash for the truck. The rest of the signing money went into a savings account.

An arson investigation doesn't require the urgency of responding to a fire, so on his way, Thomas stopped at a donut shop that never closed. He only intended to buy a large cup of coffee to help wake himself up, but the smell of fresh-baked apple fritters was hard to resist. The baker behind the counter knew him well.

"Good morning, Tom! Another case?"

"Yeah, why do they always happen on a weekend and after midnight?"

With coffee in hand and a fresh apple fritter on the seat next to him, Thomas headed to the fire scene.

On arrival, Thomas saw that an engine company and the Battalion Chief were still on scene. The sky was still dark, and a chill in the air smacked Thomas as he got out of the truck. He pulled off his duty boots and slipped on his overalls and a pair of rubber boots that he kept stored in the bed of his truck.

Thomas' boots made slapping noises as he waded across the ground that was soaked in ash-filled water from the firefighting activity that had gone on before his arrival. The air was heavy with the smell of burnt wood, and the stench of asphalt roofing material that lingered in wisps of smoke in the night air. Thomas made his way to the command post to notify the battalion chief that he had arrived.

"Chief, I'm here. What do we have?"

"Tom, sorry to get you up this early, but this one sounds like it's going to be worth your time. Not sure about all the details, but I think you'll have police in on this one before you're done. Check with Captain Peterson, he'll have more information since he was inside the building. I haven't been in there yet."

Thomas could see from the outside that the fire had involved a warehouse structure along the east side of the street. Nothing stood out about the building except that it had no identifying marks or signs as to what kind of business it had been. The building otherwise was typical of the many small warehouses in this part of town. He noted a front office in one west-facing corner and a large roll-up door with a loading dock in the other west corner. A large window at the office area was darkened by heavy smoke-staining, and the roof had burned through above the office.

Thomas also saw that it had burned through above the main portion of the building as well. That alone made Thomas a little suspicious, because it could indicate the fire broke out in multiple locations. Thomas had already been a little suspicious of the fire when the dispatcher called. A warehouse fire that starts in a closed business on a Saturday night after midnight would send up red flags to any firefighter.

Thomas found Captain Steve Peterson in front of the building as the engine company was rolling up used fire hose.

"What's up Steve?" he asked.

"Tom, this is a weird one," the captain said. "I think we have multiple areas of origin, and you either have a victim or a suspect dead on the floor in the middle of the warehouse."

"Oh! OK ... looks like I'll be here a while then."

"Well, our fun is almost done here. The engine crew is already picking up their hose. It's your turn have some fun and get dirty, Tom."

Thomas was already taking exterior photographs as Captain Peterson spoke. Showing no emotion, he took over the fire scene with a simple, "Yeah, thanks."

Thomas noted that the large window in front of the office area was broken, and heavy smoke-staining was obvious around and above the window opening. The large roll-up door to the loading dock had a large triangle cut in it where firefighters had forced their access into the building. Thomas' investigation proceeded to the building's interior. It was constructed of concrete that had been poured on the ground and then tilted up and locked into place during construction. The floor was also concrete, so the only immediate damage observed was smoke staining. These buildings simply do not burn down. The contents burn, the interior walls burn, and the wooden roofs burn, but the concrete always remains.

The high-arched ceiling was charred and burned through in a couple of places, with the heaviest damage to and above the office area. The office walls were constructed of wood frame covered with drywall. The walls were heavily charred and discolored from floor to ceiling in some places. Close observation revealed dark discoloration in a couple of wide-spread areas of the floor, where it became quickly obvious to Thomas that a flammable liquid had pooled and then burned. The patterns on the floor seemed more consistent with an intentional widespread pour, rather than a spill.

Thomas walked into a second, larger room that connected with the office. He found what looked like a metal exam table and a metal cabinet filled with plastic bottles of chemicals. Searching through the remains of the cabinet, Thomas found many of the bottles had melted from exposure to the fire. Not knowing what the bottles contained, Thomas made note of the few labels he could read: Restoratone, A-OK, Cavicide.

Thomas moved into the warehouse portion of the building. The damage to that area was mostly just heavy smoke damage. He also noticed patterns on the concrete floor that were consistent with the burning of flammable liquid at floor level. In the vast open space of this room, little was around that would burn. A flammable liquid was the only thing that burned in that area. No ignition sources were found in close proximity to this burn pattern, which was further evidence that the fire may have been intentionally set.

Then he came upon the body of a male, face-down, near the middle of the warehouse. The body was several feet from the closest burn pattern, and the man had not been burned by the fire. He was fully clothed, and the clothing had been smoke-stained and soaked wet due to firefighting activity.

Thomas took photos of the body, then called over one of the firefighters to help turn the man over so he could examine the front of the body. He looked to be in his 80's, and his skin appeared to be bright red, much like a sunburn, likely due to exposure to the heat from the surrounding fire.

Closer observation of the face showed no signs of soot around the nose or mouth. Thomas jotted down all this information in his notebook.

"Male victim, 80's, died prior to the fire, no signs of smoke or heat inhalation."

Noticing something under the victim's shirt, Thomas pulled it up and saw electrodes on his chest. They were the same type electrodes Thomas and the other medics used often on patients they had treated for chest pain on medical calls. Thomas also noted what appeared to be a very large and poorly sutured, area near the body's right shoulder, extending down under the armpit. Thomas made a note of it and took photos, but he figured it was probably just a pacemaker surgery gone bad. Thomas deduced that this could not be the arsonist and suspected that he may well have died at another location from some sort of heart-related event or botched pacemaker operation.

Continuing the investigation, Thomas came upon a walk-in refrigerator in one corner of the warehouse. Entering the refrigerator, Thomas found three more dead bodies on metal gurneys, two males and one female, all three naked.

Thomas thought to himself, "Were these victims of some heinous crime spree?" Then he shouted out to nobody in particular, "What the hell is going on here?"

Thomas made his way to a portion of the office that had not burned badly and found a time-stamp clock and a wall rack of time cards. Four cards were on the rack, and each card had a name and a time in, but no time out. Thomas guessed that the cards must relate to the victims. Were the bodies victims of some sort of cult?

Dispatch, at the battalion chief's request, had earlier called a person who was listed as a responsible party, according to the business license. That man showed up at the fire scene around 3 a.m. and introduced himself to Thomas as Steve Douglas.

"Steve, are you the business owner?" Thomas took out his notebook.

"No, my stepdad, Harold Baker, owns the place."

"What's the name of the business?"

"Evergreen"

"What kind of business is this, and do you know the guy on the floor?"

Steve said he was just an occasional pick-up and delivery employee, and that the building was used for storage before a body was to be cremated.

"What do you know about the guy on the floor, Steve?"

"He's a customer. I checked him in last night."

"A customer?" Thomas took that to mean he was scheduled for cremation. "The chemicals in the cabinet, I'm guessing, would be for embalming then?"

"That's right, occasionally my stepdad will perform embalming if the family wants an open-casket funeral before the cremation. Another employee and I pick up bodies from hospitals and convalescent homes, then store them in the refrigerator. A card is made out for each customer, and they're clocked in."

"Why would a 'customer' be on the floor in the middle of the building?"

"That's not where he was when I checked him in around midnight." Steve seemed a little uncomfortable. "I placed the customer in the walk-in."

Steve led Thomas to what was left of the office and showed Thomas the time clock and the customer cards. The cards were wet but not burned by the fire. Thomas photographed the time cards and asked which customer had been on the floor.

"John Nash, he was a World War II veteran, I think."

A slender young man who looked to be still in his teens walked into the office.

"Hey Steve, I'm here."

"Investigator Cheshire, this is Todd Sherwood. He works with me."

Steve and Todd excused themselves to attend to the "customers" while Thomas moved on with his scene investigation. Thomas was still taking photographs and making a diagram of the building and the locations of the bodies when he noticed Steve had backed a white van into the warehouse. Steve and Todd then set about loading bodies into the van. They were placing the bodies, one at a time, onto a metal gurney. Then they rolled it over to the open van. One would hold the customer's arms, and the other would hold the legs, and they would heave the body into the van like they were loading firewood.

"Thump … bang" were the sounds heard as each "customer" landed in the van.

Thomas noted that the younger employee, Todd, would wince when he heard the noise the bodies made, while Steve seemed emotionless. Thump … bang. Thump … bang. Thump … bang. Until all "customers" were loaded into the van.

Thomas stopped Steve and asked, "Where will you be taking the bodies?"

Steve told him that they were going to a smaller facility near Los Angeles and gave Thomas the address of that location. Thomas was satisfied that the bodies were legitimate customers at that point and not victims of some heinous crime, so he allowed them to transport the bodies.

Thomas had determined very early that this had been arson with multiple of areas of origin, but no suspects had been developed yet. By the time Thomas had finished with his scene investigation, the sun was starting to come up, and the fire companies had long ago packed up and were back in their stations sleeping.

Thomas pulled a few empty paint cans from the back of his truck and re-entered the warehouse. He filled the cans with debris from different locations where he thought flammable liquid residue may have been, then tamped down the lids to seal the evidence. He next placed tamper-proof tape over the lids and noted the date, time and location they were taken from on each can. Then Thomas signed the cans and placed them in the bed of his truck.

Thomas drove home and managed to sleep for a few hours. He had the rest of the weekend off to recuperate before going into the station to follow up on this mysterious and bizarre scene investigation.

Chapter 2

Play Ball

Thomas Cheshire hadn't always wanted to be a firefighter. He was raised in Redondo Beach, California, where he lived with his father, a Hughes aerospace engineer, his stay-at-home mother and a younger sister.

Thomas grew up listening to the music of the Beach Boys because his father played their music often and told stories about his early involvement in the band as a roadie. Thomas' dad once drove through the old Hawthorne neighborhood, pointing out where his house had been and where the Beach Boys' home had stood.

A small historical plaque marked a spot close to where that house had stood, but now a freeway ran through the area. Thomas' father liked to say, "Seems like nothing ever stays the same." Thomas would find out how true those words were years later.

While other kids were listening to Guns N' Roses and Iron Maiden, Thomas enjoyed the sounds of that old local band, the same Beach Boys his father had listened to and had been neighborhood friends with while growing up. The tunes spoke to Thomas and to the way of life he enjoyed, and of course the beach, which he loved. Thomas could almost feel the wind in his face, the sand under his toes and taste of the salty air whenever he was listening to their music.

Whenever Thomas couldn't hitch a ride to the beach from the older boys in the neighborhood, he would ride his bike. Thomas fashioned a trailer for his surfboard out of PVC pipe and a couple of old wheelbarrow wheels. He enjoyed surfing the beaches of Torrance and Redondo. He was a beach rat, he used the term with pride, and he came to know most of the other regulars up and down the beach. Occasionally he would sneak into Palos Verdes to surf until the local surf gangs would run him off for not being a local.

Thomas' first job in public service was as a lifeguard, serving the Torrance beaches during summer months of his high school days. However, Thomas dreamed of being a professional basketball player or a major league pitcher someday.

Thomas was not a remarkable student, but he did excel in sports, especially basketball and baseball. He enjoyed Little League Baseball and Pony League, achieving all-star status at both levels. Thomas also joined the Junior Lifeguard program by the time he was 11 years old.

At 6-foot-2, he made varsity in both sports in his sophomore year. During his senior year, his school basketball team ended the season 17-2, and Thomas made the all-league team. In baseball, Thomas finished the season with six wins and no losses. He carried a batting average of .451 with three home runs. He made all-league in baseball as well, while his team went 18-3 on the season.

Around this same time, a young girl named Amber caught Thomas' eye. Amber was a junior on the cheer squad during Thomas' senior season of basketball. She was a standout on the school track team and debate team when she wasn't involved with the cheer squad. Thomas was smitten with Amber from the first time he saw her. She was tall, lean and had shoulder length, raven-colored hair. Amber was smart, and it was easy for Thomas to talk with her. The two were inseparable from the time they met.

In his senior year of high school, Thomas was heavily scouted by several major league teams. Scouts lined the fences of the school field and clocked his fastball at 92 mph. Thomas also had a strong curveball that found the corners of the plate. Thomas even threw a no-hitter and racked up 90 strikeouts during his senior year.

Thomas was offered full scholarships from Arizona State and Long Beach State University to play baseball; and the University of California/Irvine to play basketball. He was eventually drafted by the Seattle Mariners in the third round.

Along with his mom and dad, Thomas sat down at the dinning room table to view the pros and cons of each offer. Thomas was leaning toward Long Beach State. They had a good baseball program, and it was close to home. The thought was, if he excelled at Long Beach State, he might be drafted higher next time around. The decision was made, and Thomas signed a letter of intent to attend Long Beach State in the fall.

Before classes could start at Long Beach State, the Mariners called, wanting to make one last offer to sign Thomas before the school year started. Thomas sat in the living room with his mom, dad and girlfriend, Amber, to talk with the Mariners' representative. The Mariners' rep told Thomas how much they believed in him and went into detail about their farm system. He also assured them that they thought Thomas would progress through the system quickly. The representative slid an offer sheet across the coffee table. The team had upped their signing bonus to $425,000. That was enough to persuade Thomas to sign with the Mariners and forgo his education.

The Mariners left with a contract in hand. The family celebrated with hugs all around. Thomas was about to start his dream job. It wasn't long before Thomas had a check in hand and instructions to report to a rookie league team in Arizona.

A new Chevy Silverado 1500 truck was the first order of business. Thomas went down to the dealership and paid cash for the truck. It was a beauty, jet black with shiny chrome rims. The rest of Thomas' signing money went into a savings account.

Thomas packed his bags and bid farewell, leaving his parents, sister and Amber, waving good-by from his parents' front lawn. He was off, headed to Arizona for the rookie league in his new truck.

Once in Arizona, Thomas was given a monthly salary of $800 plus meal money. Many of the Rookie League season-ticket holders hosted the rookie players. Thomas was given a list of team boosters who were willing to house players for the season. The team urged Thomas to contact the Edwards family for housing.

Bob and Laurie Edwards, were big baseball fans and offered room and board to a rookie player each season for $100 a month. Bob worked for the Phoenix Fire Department as a captain and had been a season-ticket holder for many years. He and Laurie watched as many of the Arizona Mariners games as they could.

The Edwards were old hands at this and were able to fill Thomas in on what to expect during his first season. Thomas and the Edwards became fast friends, and the couple became like second parents to Thomas. Laurie Edwards would make sure Thomas' uniforms were clean for game time and always had a warm meal for him, even on the days Bob was working his shift at the fire station.

Thomas had success right away, posting a 6-1 record and an ERA of 1.24 in the Arizona rookie league. Thomas threw two shutouts during the season. His parents and Amber made the trip to Arizona a few times during the season to watch him play. They even managed to be in attendance when he threw one of his shutouts.

At the end of the season, Thomas thanked the Edwards' and bid them farewell, naively asking if he could stay with them next season.

"You're always welcome here, Tom," Bob Edwards replied, "but I think you'll be playing somewhere else next season."

Thomas spent the off-season weight training and trying to strengthen his arm. He also spent time surfing the waves of Torrance and Redondo. The smell of the salt air and the wind in his face made Thomas feel free. Surfing was relaxing and helped him think more clearly whenever something was troubling him. Thomas saw Amber as much as he could, now that she, too, had graduated from high school, but they had to schedule that time around her job as a grocery checker.

Captain Edwards was right. As the next season rolled around, Thomas found himself in Washington playing for another Mariners minor-league team, the AquaSox, and another host family had a room for him.

In Thomas' third start of the season, he was facing the Boise Hawks. The AquaSox led 2-1 in the fifth inning when Thomas delivered a fastball that was wildly outside. Thomas heard a pop as the ball left his hand. He dropped his glove and bent over in pain, a sharp and searing pain in his right elbow. It was almost unbearable. His elbow started to swell, and his fingers began to tingle.

Thomas was about to realize that his second season of professional baseball had just ended. The team doctor looked at the injury and had the elbow iced immediately. The doc prescribed Oxycodone for the pain and scheduled Thomas for an MRI the next morning. Thomas didn't understand much of what the doctor was telling him, but understood enough when he heard the doctor say, "Tom, you blew your arm out. I'm afraid you're done for the season."

When Thomas awoke the next morning, his elbow had a deep black bruise, and had swollen, making his elbow appear almost twice its original size. The MRI revealed that he had torn ligaments. Surgery would be required, and he would be out for at least a year. Thomas made the trip home to Southern California, where he was scheduled for reconstructive surgery to repair his elbow, a surgery commonly known as Tommy John surgery, named after the former Los Angeles Dodger pitcher who was the first to undergo the procedure.

Thomas had been taking the Oxycodone for a while. Long enough to know he didn't like it because it made him sleepy and gave him stomach pain. After the surgery, Thomas' arm was placed in a brace for two weeks before he was even allowed to move his elbow; he was finally allowed to remove his brace after the fifth week.

He had a long recovery ahead of him. Thomas endured three months of physical therapy before he felt like he had full range of motion back. Next he had to work on his grip and further strengthen his arm. It would be almost a year before Thomas was allowed to throw off a mound again.

Thomas worked out with his old high school coach, pitching batting practice to the high school students, until he felt comfortable returning to competitive baseball. The Mariners had been following Thomas' progress and felt it was time for him to rejoin the AquaSox. Thomas drove to Everett, Washington, in anticipation of joining the team during their second month of the season.

He took the mound in front of the coaches during a practice session, but the radar gun showed he wasn't able to throw with the same velocity. He had also lost some control of his curveball. The Mariners were patient with Thomas as they tried to work with him on his strength, speed and control. Near the end of the season, Thomas got a chance to come into a game in relief. He got shelled, walking one and giving up four hits without recording an out. The next morning, the team released Thomas, effectively ending his career before it started.

He was broken-hearted, having been told, and believing, for years that he was destined for the majors and possibly even a Hall-of-Fame career. Thomas loaded up his truck and made the trip back to Southern California, a drive that seemed much longer going home than it had when he drove up just a few weeks prior.

Uncertain what to do next, Thomas used some of his signing bonus savings and rented an apartment near the beach in Southern California. He had no long-term plans at that point, other than to surf as much as he could. Thomas was seeing Amber almost every day, but he seemed to have no direction for what to do next with his life.

He had turned into a beach bum. He let his hair grow out and went days without shaving. He knew that the signing bonus money would only take him so far and that he needed direction. If he was going to make it in life, he needed to change.

Chapter 3

A Different Calling

Thomas remembered the long talks and kindness of Captain Edwards and his wife Laurie, his host from when he played rookie ball for the Phoenix Mariners. He also remembered visiting a Phoenix fire station and how the firefighters reminded him of his baseball teammates. Thomas began to think about the fire department as a possible occupational option.

He called Captain Edwards, and told him how he had blown out his arm and how he was struggling about what to do with his life.

"I know," Bob said, "we were following your career and hoping to see that you would make it back into baseball. Laurie and I are glad that you are well otherwise ... Tom, have you ever thought about being a firefighter?"

Tom's eyes lit up. "Yes, that's one of the reasons I called you. It looked like fun and something I might be able to do."

Captain Edwards went on to tell Thomas how to become a firefighter and the training he could expect. Immediately after his conversation with Captain Edwards, Thomas cut his shoulder-length hair, shaved and drove his truck over to El Camino College, where he enrolled in the Fire Science program. Within two years, Thomas had graduated from El Camino College with a degree in Fire Science and had gone through a college-sponsored fire academy.

Thomas remembered Captain Edwards telling him the odds might be long in landing a job with a fire department, since sometimes over 2,000 candidates would apply at a time. He was undeterred, knowing he was still in shape and had some education behind him now. Thomas starting applying to every department that offered a test.

The tests began with a written exam. Those passing the written exam moved on to a physical agility test, which further pared the candidates down. Those who remained would go on to a panel interview, and a "hire list" was formulated from those remaining candidates.

Amber, Thomas' long-time girlfriend had moved in with him by then. Any free time Thomas had, was still spent surfing. Just a few months after his graduation from El Camino College, Thomas got a callback for a chiefs interview. Against long odds, he had been hired by the fire department.

The fire academy was a little more than three months long. Thomas learned about fire ground procedures and tactics. He also learned about fire prevention and was taught emergency medical techniques. Thomas seemed to have no trouble at all and enjoyed it thoroughly, reminding him of his spring training days. The arm that couldn't pitch anymore posed no problem in using tools and dragging hose lines.

Thomas' parents and his girlfriend Amber attended the graduation ceremony. When it came time for the badge pinning, he had chosen Amber to come up and pin on his badge. The two of them posed for a photograph. Then Thomas got down on one knee, ring in hand, and proposed to Amber to great cheers and applause from the other graduates and the attendees. After a stunned moment, Amber blurted out, "YES!"

The chief shook Thomas' hand and congratulated him, then shook Amber's hand. "Welcome to the family of firefighters, Amber."

Thomas' first shift was the very next day. He had been assigned to Station 2, working for Captain Osborne, who was also the department's chaplain. Captain Osborne trained Thomas every shift during his probationary year — hose lays, vehicle extraction, medical procedures, roof operations, fire prevention, water sources and area familiarization.

Thomas went on a few calls every shift out of Station 2. He was amazed at the extent of teamwork that went into each call. The firehouse atmosphere reminded him so much of when he was a ballplayer.

He didn't have to wait long before he responded to his first fire call. During his third shift, Engine 2 was toned out for a house fire. It was midday, and when they arrived on scene, Thomas could see flames rolling out of two back windows where he presumed a bedroom might be.

Captain Osborne called for 200 feet of inch-and-a-half line to be extended to the front door. Once Thomas and Captain Osborne were gloved up and had their breathing apparatus masks in place, Thomas advanced the hose into the dwelling, with Captain Osborne behind him, moving him forward.

They advanced down the hall, hunched down to get below the dark smoke that had banked down to about 3 feet above floor level. The heat had become very intense near the doorway to a bedroom, so Thomas and Captain Osborne were now on their stomachs. Thomas opened the bale on the hose line, spraying water around the ceiling and walls of the bedroom.

The air turned into a hot steam, and Thomas could feel his coat becoming heavier with the water that was settling on it. The glow of the fire soon dimmed as the fire was pushed back toward the now-broken windows. Thomas was ecstatic. He had put out his first fire, just as he had learned in training.

He felt a tingle of excitement and knew he had made the right career choice. Blowing his arm out may have been a gift from God, leading him in a different direction. Thomas couldn't wait to get back to the station to call Amber and his parents to tell them what it was like.

However, he would have to wait, because they were toned out on a traffic collision before they got back to the station. Then, of course, upon returning to the station, Thomas had to change out a few lengths of dirty fire hose, wash the fire engine and his turnouts, fill the breathing apparatus tanks and then shower up.

The first year seemed to pass quickly. The date for his wedding had been set for the weekend after his probation ended. Many of the members from his shift attended the wedding ceremony held at the Saddleback Church. Thomas and his high school sweetheart, now wife, Amber, felt like they were on top of the world. The Cheshires, both having time off coming to them, flew to Cancun for their honeymoon.

They were very happy with their jobs and enjoyed what being part of the fire department family had brought to their life. Thomas loved his new job and got along with all the other firefighters. He especially liked the light-hearted kidding the firefighters engaged in. The camaraderie and teamwork reminded him so much of the baseball teams on which he had played.

Thomas and Amber took vacations with a few of the firefighters families. They went dirt biking together at Red Rock, water skiing on the Colorado River, snow skiing at Squaw Valley and took couples trips to Palm Springs and Las Vegas.

Thomas was asked to join the department's softball team, an offer at which he gladly jumped at. He could not have expected this life a few years prior when the Mariners let him go. Thomas, sadly, could not foresee what tragedies would befall him.

Chapter 4

Tough Day at the Office

A few years later in the Cheshire's suburban Southern California home, it was barely 6 a.m. when the phone woke Thomas from a dead sleep. He quickly fumbled for the phone so as to not wake Amber.

Thomas whispered, "Hello?"

"Firefighter Cheshire, this is Captain Clarke, you are ordered back to headquarters station to work an overtime spot today."

"Yes sir, I'll be right in," he whispered.

Manpower had been a problem at that time. In an effort to replace recently retired members of the department, a few new hires were still in the academy. However, the manning problem had been compounded by the fact that the department had an engine dispatched to Central California as part of a wildfire strike-team. Many fires were burning across the state that season, and that was the second time one of their engines had been called away in the last two months.

Thomas quietly dressed, kissed Amber on the cheek and whispered, "I'm sorry babe, I've been ordered back to work today."

On his way out, he opened the doors to his children's rooms. The twins, Wendy and Michael, were both sleeping soundly. Thomas quietly closed each of their doors and made his way to his truck and headed out to headquarters station.

The sky was clear, and it appeared that it would eventually be another typically bright and sunny Southern California day. Thomas, a firefighter/paramedic for seven years by then, reported to headquarters for the mandatory 24-hour shift with the crew of B shift on that day. Headquarters housed Engine 1, Truck 1, Medic 1 and Battalion Chief 1.

Walking through the apparatus room, he saw the white magnetic board hanging on the wall. It read "B Shift Duty, Captain Jimi Roberts, Engineer Jared Michaels, Firefighter Dave Scott Engine 1; Captain Bill Davis, Engineer Steve Peterson, Firefighter Tom Cheshire Truck 1; Paramedics Crystal Collins and Ken Barry Medic 1." Tom's assignment for the shift would be the truck.

Thomas thought, optimistically, to himself, "This is going to be a great shift." Thomas enjoyed working with Captain Davis and Engineer Peterson in the past, and he wasn't going to have to work on the paramedic unit that day.

Thomas gathered his turnout jacket, pants, boots and helmet, placing them in the jump seat he was assigned to that day. He then checked out his breathing apparatus to make sure it was working properly and topped off with air. Satisfied, Thomas made his way to the kitchen. Thomas poured a cup of coffee and joined the other "off-going" and "on-coming" firefighters around the table. Everyone was chatting about what had happened the shift before, and Thomas visited with firefighters he had known, and even vacationed with, for years by then.

When 0800 hours (8 a.m.) rolled around, the only firefighters remaining around the table were the ones assigned to work the B shift that day, along with a couple of firefighters still trying to wake up from a tough shift the night before.

Captain Bill Davis, a slightly graying, husky and grizzled veteran with almost 30 years on the job, was chewing on an unlit cigar butt. He went over the day's planned activities.

"Engine 1 and Medic 1 will be out on fire prevention inspections this morning, Truck Crew is cooking today, and it will be all hands for two tours of school children in the afternoon." A fairly typical day for the headquarters station.

At the end of Captain Davis' announcements, Thomas had one of his own.

"We just found out Amber is pregnant again."

Captain Davis, pulling the cigar from his face, smiled. "Congratulations, I see cigars on the back porch in our future ... All right everyone, let's play safe out there today!"

After a light workout session consisting of weights and treadmill time, the crew showered and dressed into their duty uniforms. Over the station PA speaker, Captain Davis bellowed, "Truck 1, saddle up, store run. Engine 1, Medic 1, out on prevention."

The truck was excused from inspections because the Engineer, Steve Peterson, was the duty cook for the shift. Engineer Peterson finished collecting chow money from each of the firefighters, then took the truck out of the apparatus room and made his way to Safeway for groceries.

Steve and Thomas were filling their shopping basket with groceries needed for lunch and dinner while Captain Davis stayed with the truck. Halfway through the shopping, the dispatcher could be heard over the radio as she toned out, "Headquarters, Station 2 ... Engine 1, Truck 1, Medic 1, Battalion 1, Engine 2 ... Structure fire, 6143 Crosby Street, time out 10:26."

The basket of food was abandoned in the produce section as Thomas and Engineer Peterson raced back to the truck. Captain Davis was already in his turnouts and heading back into the cab of the truck. Engineer Peterson and Thomas jumped into their turnout pants and boots, donned their jackets, fire hoods and helmets; then headed out to the Crosby Street address. The air packs were cinched up, and masks hung around their necks while en-route. Still a mile out still, the crew could see a tall column of black smoke rising straight up in the distance.

Captain Davis picked up the mike and reported, "Truck 1, smoke showing, working fire."

Battalion Chief Raymond Mendoza, still en-route, began giving out assignments.

"Engine 1, fire attack, Engine 2, exposures. Truck 1, ventilation, Medic 1, rescue and utilities." Chief Mendoza took a deep breath and continued, "I will be known as Crosby IC (Incident Command)."

Truck 1 was first to arrive, and Captain Davis, cigar still in his mouth, reported, "Truck 1 on scene, two-story single-family dwelling with fire showing from a second floor, east facing, window, no immediate exposures."

Engine 1 was next to arrive, and Captains William's crew began stretching hose lines from the engine to the doorway. Captain Davis led Thomas and Engineer Peterson to the structure with a 35-foot extension ladder. The ladder was strategically placed at a corner of the building, close to the where the fire was burning.

Engineer Peterson grabbed a rubbish hook from the truck, while Thomas grabbed a chain saw. The three firefighters made their way up the ladder. On the roof, engineer Peterson pounded his rubbish hook on the shingled roof, looking for solid place to walk on. The rubbish hook thumped down with a loud "thud" every foot or so along the way until Captain Davis was satisfied that the spot appeared to be right over the fire. Engineer Peterson peeled back shingles with the rubbish hook to expose the wood-covered roof. Thomas began his first cut with the chainsaw, and smoke began seeping out.

The noise, smoke and flames attracted the attention of neighbors, who formed a large crowd near the building. Thomas had not finished the first cut in the roof when, suddenly, the entire roof structure failed. Captain Davis, Engineer Peterson and Thomas all disappeared through the roof and into the dwelling. Gasps and screams went up from the onlookers. One female onlooker started screaming, "Get them! Get them! Get the firemen!"

Captain Davis, Engineer Peterson and Thomas were all sliding down the roof toward the structure's interior, right toward the fire. Their backs were slammed up against the air packs they were wearing as they slid down the roof toward the flames.

It seemed like an eternity to Thomas as he slid into the abyss. When the sliding came to a stop, Captain Davis lay unconscious in a heap to Thomas' left. Engineer Peterson was to Thomas' right side, sitting up, moving his arms and moaning. Thomas felt a sharp pain to his lower back. It felt like he had been cracked in the back by a lightning bolt. His left leg started to go numb, and through his gloves he could feel the heat from the fire below him, which was already causing the asphalt shingles to melt and blister.

Captain Williams' Engine 1 crew, backed up by the crew of Medic 1, made their way to the second floor with hose lines. With the roof having failed, visibility was no longer a problem. The smoke had dissipated, and the roof now lay in a heap on the second floor. The fire crews had plenty of available light with the roof missing. The engine and medic crews were able to toss aside broken portions of the roof to make a quick knock-down of the fire before it got to the crew of Truck 1.

Captain Davis had regained consciousness but seemed dazed and confused as to where he was. He complained of pain to his right knee. The medics removed Captain Davis' turnout coat and cut his uniform pants to reveal a badly dislocated right knee.

Thomas complained of back pain when the medics reached him. Thomas' coat was gently slid off, and he was placed in a cervical collar, then strapped to a backboard before being removed from the building.

Engineer Peterson had a great deal of pain in his left lower leg. His turnout pants were cut away to reveal an obviously broken leg. His leg was placed in a traction splint, and he, too, was removed from the scene.

All three firefighters were rushed to Harbor General Hospital, where Captain Davis was treated for a concussion and a dislocated right knee. He endured months of physical therapy. Captain Davis never return to work and applied for retirement three months after the fire.

Engineer Peterson went on to recover from a broken femur and broken collar bone. Engineer Peterson returned to work as captain, replacing Captain Davis.

Thomas, on the other hand, had a broken back, between his fifth lumbar spine and his first sacral spine. Thomas' injury was due to the air pack slamming up against his back as he slid into the fire. Thomas was the only one admitted to the hospital on that day, pending surgery.

Battalion Chief Mendoza met the three firefighters at the hospital and was updated on their condition. The chief then called the families of Captain Davis and Engineer Peterson to fill them in on what had happened and their condition. Battalion Chief Mendoza knew that with Thomas being admitted to the hospital, he needed to deliver the news of the accident to Amber in person.

Chapter 5

Tragic News

Thomas' home was a few miles outside of city limits where Amber, his wife of six years, and twins Wendy and Michael, age four, were going about their day. Battalion Chief Mendoza had just found out that morning that Amber was pregnant again and thought it was important to make the drive down the freeway to inform Amber of Thomas' injury in person, rather than call her.

Chief Mendoza parked the shiny, red command vehicle in front of the home and made the long walk up the driveway to the front door. The Battalion Chief took a deep breath, then knocked on the door. When Amber opened the door, she screamed, "Nooo!"

Chief Mendoza grabbed Amber by her shoulders just as her knees begin to buckle. The battalion chief quickly reassured her.

"It's not what you think. Tom is OK, he's awake and alert, he is expected to make a full recovery, and he wasn't burned. A roof failed, and he hurt his back at a fire this morning."

Amber slumped onto the sofa, still a little overwhelmed by the news. Battalion Chief Mendoza then offered Amber a ride to the hospital. Amber, having regained her composure, declined.

"With the child seats, it will be a hassle and I'll need a way home anyway, so I'll drive myself. Could you do me a favor though chief, and call his parents? If they could meet me at the hospital, they'll be able to help with the children while we take turns visiting with Tom."

"Absolutely, and if there's anything else we can do for you, don't hesitate to call any of us."

"Thanks, chief."

Amber, quickly and calmly, buckled Wendy and Michael into the back seat of her mini-van for the trip to the hospital. Being mid-day, the freeway traffic was unusually light. Amber's mind was on Thomas when Wendy began to fuss in the back seat. Amber turned around to hand Wendy a stuffed animal that was on the floor. When Amber turned back around, to her horror, she realized that the traffic in front of her had come to a complete stop. It was too late for her to stop. Before she could even apply the brakes, her mini-van plowed into the back of an eighteen-wheeler. A second car then slammed into the back of Amber's vehicle.

Arriving firefighters could not save Amber. She died immediately in the twisted wreckage. Her body had to be extricated from what was left of the vehicle with the Jaws-of-Life. Michael, too, was killed in the accident. Fire crews extricated Wendy and rushed her to Harbor General Hospital with massive head and chest injuries. Medics passed an airway and strapped Wendy to a backboard.

En route to the hospital, Wendy slipped into traumatic cardiac arrest. By the time the medics rushed her into the pediatric emergency room, they were preforming CPR on her tiny body. Doctors were not able to get a blood pressure or reestablish a heart beat. Wendy was pronounced dead within minutes of her arrival at the hospital. Thomas wasn't even aware that his family had been wiped out in an accident.

He was resting comfortably in an upstairs room, feeling no pain. Dr. Hudson, the admitting doctor, had Thomas on a Dilaudid IV drip to offset the back pain. Thomas had been instructed to just use a push button to deliver the meds automatically whenever the pain became unbearable. The device had been set so that meds could be delivered only once an hour, to avoid overdosing, no matter how many times Thomas pushed the button.

Dr. Hudson had been the attending doctor who tried to save Thomas' daughter, Wendy, as well. After pronouncing Wendy's death, he summoned captain Derek Osborne, the fire department chaplain, and both gathered in Thomas' room to deliver the tragic news.

Amber's parents were already in Thomas' room at the time. The doctor introduced himself to the group while the chaplain grabbed Thomas' hand. The doctor stood at the foot of the bed, next to Amber's parents, and delivered the tragic news.

Amber's mother gave out a shriek, Thomas mindlessly pushed down the medicine delivery button to self-administer more pain meds. Closing his eyes without a word, a tear rolled down Thomas' cheek. There was enough Dilaudid to kill the back pain, but there would never be enough medicine in the world to dull the pain Thomas felt then.

The next day, Thomas was scheduled for surgery through his abdomen to remove broken portions of his lumbar and sacral spine. Three days later, a second surgery was performed through his back to insert two rods, six screws and cadaver bone. The surgery fused portions of his spinal column together.

While Thomas was in the hospital, he had a steady stream of firefighters come to check up on him. They brought flowers and books to read. Bill Wilder, a fire academy buddy, snuck in a couple of beers that they shared.

"I am so sorry for your loss, Tom. Is there anything I can do for you to make your life any easier, buddy?"

"Yeah, Bill you can. Can you take care of the details for a Celebration of Life ceremony for Amber and kids?"

"No problem, I'll make it happen. It will be nice."

"And don't forget ... we were expecting another baby in a few months."

"No problem, Tom. I got you covered brother."

Visitors made the days seem short, but the nights were always long. Thomas awoke many times due to the pain. He hit his button to self-administer pain meds, then would drift off to sleep once again.

On the fifth day, Tom was released to go home with a system of timed-released pain medication taped to his side. Arriving home, Thomas found only loneliness and sorrow. Amber, Wendy and Michael ... and the baby ... all gone. Toys still littered the living room, and on the kitchen counter were two dried-out, half-eaten peanut butter and jelly sandwiches and two cups of curdled milk. Thomas could do little more than lie in bed and struggle to make it to the bathroom during the first few days home.

After four days, Bill came to drive Thomas to the doctors' office for a follow-up visit. The doctor, satisfied with how Thomas had healed, removed the pain medicine infusion system. All Thomas had for comfort now was a prescription for Oxycodone that the doctor was sending home with him. Thomas was a little leery, remembering the time he had taken this medicine while he was recovering from his old baseball injury, years ago.

Thomas' back injury was painful with every movement, and he struggled to get around with the use of a walker. When the day came for the Celebration of Life, Thomas was able to get around with a cane. Bill picked up Thomas for the trip to the church. It was a long and silent trip, as neither man spoke.

It was a nice celebration, held at the same Saddleback Church where Thomas and Amber were married. It didn't seem that long ago to Thomas. In attendance were Amber's parents, Thomas' parents, a couple dozen friends and family members, along with most of Thomas' co-workers. A single bagpiper played Amazing Grace while the attendees filed out of the church.

Many of Thomas' co-workers took turns looking in on him from time to time, to have a beer with him and ask if they could do anything for him.

As time passed, Thomas became noticeably thinner and he had not shaved since the Celebration of Life. Word got out about

Thomas' condition, and some of the firefighters began bringing lunches and dinners for him. Some of the meals went uneaten and began to fill the refrigerator.

The fire department chaplain, Derek Osborne, paid Thomas a visit and was able to give him some encouraging words about life and carrying on as a tribute to Amber, Wendy, Michael and their unborn child. The chaplain was of some help but, when he left, he knew Thomas still struggled with a double dose of pain ... the loss of his family and the severe damage in his back.

Chapter 6

Light Duty

Eight weeks passed, over which Thomas spent most of his time split between physical therapy and just sitting in his house watching television. Able to drive by himself by then, he reported to the doctor's office for a check-up and a progress report on his recovery.

Thomas had been getting around without the walker or cane for a bit, but when he returned to the doctor's office; however, his movements were still stiff and painful.

"How does the back feel, Thomas?" The doctor seemed concerned.

"I can move around on my own better, but it still hurts. Still real stiff."

"I'm going to give you the go ahead to work, but only light duty for now. And here's a renewal on your pain meds."

In truth, Thomas had not been in severe pain for a couple of weeks, but the Oxycodone helped numb him from the deaths of his entire family. It also helped him sleep. The pain meds left his mouth dry, so he kept a bottle of water nearby. The medicine had a side effect that gave him lingering pain, like shards of glass in his stomach, so he took Tums a few times during the day.

He returned to Headquarters station the next morning and approached Fire Chief Clayborne to tell him that the doctor had released him for light duty. Thomas outwardly appeared to be much thinner and had about two months worth of whiskers on his face. The chief told Thomas that there was an opening in the Fire Investigation Unit that Thomas might want to pursue.

"Tom, it's Friday, why don't you come in Monday morning and report to Captain Thompson? But first you're going to have to shave that thing off your face, and a haircut wouldn't hurt, either."

Thomas was glad to get out of the house and needed to find a way to stop all this tragedy from incapacitating him. Getting back to work might help.

"Yes sir, of course. Thank you," Thomas said. "I look forward to getting back here."

On Monday morning, Thomas reported to Captain Ed Thompson of the Investigation Unit. Thomas' job began with reading and then filing fire reports from the previous week. Whenever a fire occurred within the city, Captain Thompson took Thomas with him to go over the process of fire scene investigation and interview techniques. Thomas sometimes took an Oxycodone, just to make it through his work day.

The medicine tended to make Thomas a little drowsy, so he spent his lunch hour in the day room, sleeping in an easy chair. When he woke, he always had Tums and a bottle of water with him to fight the dry mouth and stomach pains.

Thomas threw himself into the job, enrolling in state-sanctioned mini-courses that would help certify him in fire and explosion investigations. Thomas even took weapons training in preparation for carrying a weapon. A few months went by, and Thomas' physical pain was just an old memory, but he continued his use of the pain medication simply to dull his suffering for the loss of his family. No matter how much he threw himself into his work, that pain never faded.

Thomas, usually a very positive and energetic guy, had become noticeably short-tempered and sullen most of the time. Captain Thompson and the other firefighters tried to overlook Thomas' moods, thinking that it surely was due to him losing his family, and that he would get over it in time. His fellow firefighters, once his best friends, started keeping their distance. Thomas had become an outsider, the "arson guy" who carried a gun and no longer did shift work.

When Thomas' Oxycodone medication ran out, he made an appointment with his doctor.

"Thomas, I'm going to fill your prescription again," the doctor said, "but I want you to use it sparingly. You need to start backing off. I'm also going to release you back to full duty."

Thomas made an appointment with Chief Clayborne to tell him that he had been released for full duty.

"Tom, do you want to go back to a Medic Unit," the chief asked, "or stay on with the Investigation Unit?"

"I find the work exciting and rewarding, sir. I would like to stay on as an Investigator for the time being, if I could."

"Sure. Captain Thompson needs the help, and he tells me you're doing a fine job."

Thomas knew that working on the Investigation Unit had helped him forget his pain sometimes, and on occasions when the memory of his family crept back in, he would just take his Oxycodone, unnoticed by the other firefighters. Thomas was in a dark place, just trying to put one foot in front of the other, one day at a time, but he couldn't see that.

He decided that the Investigation Unit was going to be his assignment from now on. Just a few months later, a warehouse fire on Canyon Road sent his life spinning once again.

Chapter 7

Follow-up

On the Monday morning after he was called to the Canyon Road warehouse fire, Thomas was in the station kitchen and poured a strong cup of coffee. None of the firefighters said much to him that morning, as it appeared Thomas was his usual grumpy and moody self. He made his way to Fire Chief Clayborne's office and give him details of the fire that had occurred over the weekend. Thomas then retreated to his small, dark office.

In preparation for a trip to the Los Angeles County Sheriff's Laboratory, Thomas boxed up the paint cans of evidence that he had collected at the fire scene.

He had learned the owner to the warehouse was Harold Baker, so that was the first call of the day, since he had not been able to contact him on the day of the fire.

"Mr. Baker, this is Investigator Cheshire with the fire department. I'm sorry for your loss. Do you have time for some questions?"

"I'm devastated by the news of the fire," Baker said flatly.

"We tried to reach you at the time of the fire, but your step-son, Steve, was able to help me a little."

"Yes, thank you. Steve called me. I was in Arizona on business when the fire occurred."

"I didn't see a name on the building. What's the name of your business?"

"Evergreen Services."

According to Baker, business had been good, and he was insured for the loss through the Tushman Insurance Group.

"Do you have any enemies or any reason why someone would do this to your business?"

"No one is mad at me that I know of," Baker said. "The customers don't complain anyway ... I just warehouse the dead."

Thomas didn't find humor in that.

"That part of town has gangs, you know," Baker continued. "The Bloods and Crips. I was at the building one night and found a couple of guys in the parking lot drinking beer. I had to run them off by showing them my gun. I'm licensed to carry concealed."

Thomas was aware of the gang problem in the city because, as a paramedic, he responded to numerous shootings and drug overdoses in the past.

After finishing the call with Baker, Thomas called Detective Bob Killian with the police department. Thomas knew him from when Bob worked street patrol. He had run into Bob during Thomas' time on the Medic Unit. They had run traffic accidents, overdoses and shootings together. Bob was now assigned to the Detective Division as a part of the gang unit at the time.

"Hey Bob, it's Tom. I'm working the warehouse fire from early Saturday morning. The owner tells me that he has chased away gang members from his property in the past. Have you noticed any increased activity in that area?"

"No, not anywhere near that street. We did have that rash of stolen, stripped and burned autos on the east side."

"Yeah, I'm aware of those. That case is still sitting on my desk."

"Well, other than the kid you and I put away for setting dumpsters on fire, it's been quiet," Bob said. "I can tell you that drug activity is up in the north end of town, but I can't say for sure that gang activity had anything to do with it. I mean, I have my suspicions about the gangs being used to sell the stuff, but nothing concrete yet."

"Thanks, Bob. If you hear anything, let me know."

Thomas grabbed the box of fire debris evidence and made the long drive over to the Sheriff's Laboratory. Thomas checked the evidence into the laboratory, instructed that they check it for flammable liquid residue. The test results would take a few days to come back. Thomas knew this was just a formality, since he could tell, without the aid of a test, that the samples smelled like gasoline.

Tuesday morning came, and Thomas finally had a chance to catch up on reading the fire reports from the previous weekend. Seeing nothing of interest, Thomas found himself thinking about the Evergreen warehouse fire again.

Thomas called Steve Douglas, the stepson and employee he had met at the fire scene on the night of the fire.

"Steve, this is Investigator Cheshire, is this a good time to talk?"

"Sure, I'm not working now."

"Can you tell me what your working arrangement is?"

"Well, like I said that night, my stepdad is kind of a one-man show. He does the skilled labor, but he can't pick up the customers by himself. When he gets notification of a new customer, he calls Todd and I to do the pick-up and delivery. Sometimes we will take a customer to a funeral, then bring them back to the warehouse. That's pretty much all there is to it."

"When were you last in the building?"

"Like I said that night, I checked in a customer around midnight, then left."

"Do you remember seeing anyone in the area who didn't seem to fit? Anything resembling gang members gathering?"

"No, it's usually a quiet street, especially when we make late-night drop-offs. On that night, I did see one person walking and pushing a shopping basket. You know, like a homeless person? There are a few people that sleep on the streets near there."

"What did this person look like?"

"A white male, about 60, I would guess, thin with shaggy, gray hair. I see him from time to time."

"Can you tell me where your 'customers' come from?"

"They mostly come from Southern California convalescent hospitals, rest homes and hospitals, but occasionally we will get some from an assisted living home in Arizona."

"Where did the customer, John Nash, come from?"

"We picked him up south of Yuma, near the Mexican border, place called Villa Nueva."

Thomas thanked him for his time, then added, "Your step-dad's business was likely set on fire. So if you think of anything else, please don't hesitate to call me."

Thomas went home for the night, but he was having trouble keeping his mind occupied. He kept thinking about the Evergreen warehouse fire. Running through the possibilities: The owner had no reason to set fire to his own business, and it seem un-likely that either Steve or Todd would set fire to the place. Perhaps the place was set ablaze by gang members or the homeless man. Still, it bugged Thomas. Why would someone take a body out of the refrigerator and dump it on the floor?

Wednesday morning came, and Thomas rang up police Detective Killian.

"Bob, it's Tom again. There may have been a homeless white male with shaggy gray hair, in the area of the fire last weekend. Have your guys ever run into him?"

"Sounds like 'Old Blue.' He's been around that area for a few months. His name is Leo. Guy has got the brightest blue eyes I've ever seen. I can take you to where he hangs out if you want."

"That would be great. You got time now?"

Detective Killian picked up Thomas, and they headed out to meet Old Blue. Their first stop was the 7-Eleven store, where

Thomas picked up a deli sandwich and a pack of cigarettes. The pair then made their way to a building less than a block from the fire scene. Old Blue was found sitting under a blue tarp behind a dumpster enclosure.

Thomas approached 'Old Blue' and offered him the sandwich and cigarettes if he would come out and talk for awhile.

'Old Blue' came out from under the tarp and quickly snatched up the sandwich and the cigarettes before Thomas even introduced himself. Detective Killian had told Thomas that 'Old Blue' was 51 years old, but the man who stood before Thomas looked much older.

"Leo, my name is Tom, I work for the fire department. Could I ask you some questions?"

"Sure, but I don't know nothing about nothing."

"Leo, what's your last name?"

"Dunst, but I ain't done nothing."

" Do you remember the fire from this weekend?"

"Yup. Bad night."

"What do you mean by that?"

"You guys were making so much noise, I couldn't sleep."

"Were you anywhere near the warehouse before the fire, or did you see anyone near the building?"

"I walked by that place earlier. I remember seeing a white van and another car parked, but I didn't go near their dumpster."

"Did you see anyone in the area walking?"

"Nope!"

Thomas thanked 'Old Blue' for his time, gave him a $20 bill, and told him to spend it on dinner. Thomas knew that it would likely go toward beer.

Thomas had to hurry back to the station because he was scheduled to give a class on fire scene investigation to the crew at Station 2 after lunch. But the Evergreen warehouse case had made it hard to concentrate on anything else. Thomas was running out of people to interview.

Chapter 8

Interviews

On Thursday morning, Thomas walked into his office, cup of coffee in hand, and checked his calendar. He was scheduled to give a fire safety talk to a class of sixth graders at 10 a.m. Thomas' calendar was free after that appointment.

He finished his talk with the sixth graders and returned to his office, re-read his all his reports and went over the photographs of the Evergreen warehouse fire. The frustration of the dead-end at which Thomas found himself, led him to want to re-interview people he had already talked to.

It was after noon when Thomas called Mr. Baker back in an effort to gain more information. Thomas asked Baker where he had been at the time of the fire.

"I was in Arizona on business."

"What was the nature of that business?"

"I have one account in that state, and I was just trying to build up business in the area."

Thomas asked what his procedure was in closing up when he left that night.

"I just go out the office door and lock the door with a key."

"Who has keys to the building?"

"Just me and my stepson Steve."

"Do you have any reason to suspect either of your drivers of setting this fire?

"No, no! Not at all. But this part of the city is known to have Bloods and Crips."

"Earlier, you told me you had run a couple people off your property. Could you describe those people?"

"They were black, late teens or early 20's. One was about 6 foot and a thin mustache. The other was a little smaller and clean shaven. I think they were both under 200 pounds. They both had tattoos on their arms, but I couldn't tell you what they were."

The phone call didn't help. Thomas found himself still at a dead-end, but at least he had a description of the two young men Baker had run off his property a few days prior to the fire.

Thomas called Detective Killian again.

"Bob, I have a rough description of a couple of possible suspects in the warehouse fire. They may be gang members, so I was hoping you might know them."

Thomas described the suspects with Baker's words.

Detective Killian thought for a moment before responding. "The older one sounds like William Walker, and the younger one would be his brother Tony. They're both members of the Crips."

"Great, could you give me their contact information so I can follow up on this?"

"Yeah, well, their information won't help you, and they're not your suspects anyway, Tom."

"What do you mean?"

"They were involved in a drive-by shooting a couple of days before your fire. William is dead, took a couple of rounds to the stomach and one to the head. Tony is in the hospital still recovering from an abdominal wound. I don't have any suspects yet on that case. Typical Bloods vs. Crips gang thing. Tony won't say what happened, and no one on the street saw or heard anything, of course."

Thomas left work that night confused and frustrated that he had not been able to move the fire investigation closer to a resolution.

Friday found Thomas occupied with range time, qualifying with his 9mm semi-automatic handgun. He also had a paramedic continuing-education class and a couple of fire safety classes for grade-school kids.

Monday morning, and Thomas was back in the station. He poured his cup of coffee and grabbed a stack of fire reports from the last few days, trying to clear his mind from the Evergreen warehouse fire. Reading through the reports, he found a couple of dumpster fires, a power pole fire, and a small fire started by unattended food on a stove top.

He had trouble concentrating on the reports in front of him because his mind kept wandering back to the Evergreen warehouse fire. Then it came to him: he had not interviewed the other "customer" pick-up guy, Todd Sherwood.

Thomas checked his reports and pulled up Sherwood's phone number.

"Todd, this is Tom, the firefighter you met at the warehouse."

"Yes sir, what can I help you with?"

"How long have you worked for Mr. Baker?"

"Just a couple of months, it's really a part-time job. My cousin got me the job."

"Who's your cousin?"

"Steve. Steve got me the job. He's my cousin."

"Have you seen anyone that might be mad at your boss or your cousin?"

"No sir!"

"Do people, other than the deceased, say customers, come into the building?"

"No sir, just Mr. Baker, Steve and myself."

"Who would have keys to the business?"

"Well, Mr. Baker and Steve for sure. Maybe my aunt Cynthia, she's married to Mr. Baker now. I guess that makes him my step-uncle or something like that."

Another dead-end. It was beginning to look like this would end up as another fire that would be listed as "arson, started by person or persons unknown."

The rest of the week was filled with training and Thomas had not had the time to advance the Evergreen warehouse investigation. With the weekend coming up, Thomas thought it might be time for a road trip. Thomas knew that Chief Clayborne would never authorize a trip to Yuma, Arizona. Thomas also knew that the chief really didn't care about fire investigations. As long as the fire went out without firefighter or citizen injury, and "his" department extinguished it with as little fire loss as possible, he was happy.

Thomas would have to make this trip on his own time.

Chapter 9

Road Trip

The chief was very old-school. Just give him a report with the cause of fire, and the department's job was done, as far as he was concerned. Actually, the chief hadn't been real keen on the paramedic program, either, because when Chief Clayborne hired on, the only thing the fire department did was put out fires. "Put the wet stuff on the red stuff, and head back to the barn" is what he was fond of saying.

The chief was also known for going back and opening reports to change a fire captain's estimated dollar loss on fires, just so that the chief could report to the City Council that fire loss numbers were down on the year. For Thomas, the fIres had been more personal. Every fire was.

Saturday morning, and Thomas was off for the weekend. As soon as the sun came up, Thomas headed out for Yuma on his own time. He had packed a change of clothes in case he had to spend the night. As always, he had his water, Oxycodone and Tums in the cab of his truck.

Thomas' destination was Villa Nueva in Somerton, Arizona, 25 minutes south of Yuma. It was a beautiful day for a drive, with clear skies and temperatures in the mid 70's. Thomas' trip took him down the coast past San Clemente and Oceanside before cutting across the California desert on U.S. 8 toward the Arizona border.

Thomas rolled down the window and put in a CD of the Beach Boys, which reminded him of his youth. The beauty of the drive seemed to help Thomas keep his wife and children off his mind. He hadn't taken his Oxycodone yet on that day.

The drive took Thomas over four-and-a-half hours, and he hadn't thought through what he was wanted to achieve or what questions to ask by the time he pulled up. He just knew it was good to be out of the house, doing something other than thinking about Amber and the kids.

It was nearly noon by the time Thomas pulled up to the location. The complex was a two-story, brown stucco building sprawled out across the desert backdrop. A sign outside read "Villa Nueva, Assisted Living."

Once inside, he found a large lobby area and a reception desk. Several residents were sitting in the lobby. One was reading a newspaper, one knitting, and three others were talking to one another.

A very pretty brunette, 30-something nurse was at the reception desk. Her name tag read *"Debbie Donaldson LVN."* Thomas introduced himself and told her he was investigating a fire that may have involved someone who had been in their facility. At that point, Thomas couldn't help but notice that the nurse looked a lot like Amber.

Thomas told her about the investigation, the warehouse fire, and the dead bodies.

"Oh, how horrible ... but all of our residents are here," she said.

"This would have been a resident that passed away prior to the fire."

"Now you are just confusing me, Investigator Cheshire."

Thomas pulled out a photo of the time cards. "Do you recognize any of these names?"

"John Nash, that might have been our Johnny Nash," she said. "He was a resident here for a few years. He passed away almost two weeks ago now. It was peaceful, he passed while he was taking a nap. Wonderful gentleman, everyone loved him."

Thomas was still curious about the corpse's poorly stitched shoulder and arm pit.

"Did Mr. Nash have a pacemaker?"

"Pacemaker … um … no, Johnny had mild dementia and orthopedic issues that left him bound to a wheelchair most of the time, but no pacemaker."

"What happened to Mr. Nash after he passed away?"

"Well, I wasn't on duty when he was found, but the paramedics would have been called, then the doctor on call would have been called. The doctor would have certified Johnny's death. The desk nurse would have then called the family to see how to dispose of the remains. I know that sounds terrible, but that's how it's done."

"Could you give me the names of his family?"

"I can't do that normally, but in this case I can tell you he had no family of record."

"What do you do in that case?"

"Well, we contract with Evergreen Services, they're out of California. They come and pick up the resident and prepare them for final resting."

"Did Mr. Nash have any close friends here?"

"He was everyone's friend, but let me have you talk to Dave Conetti. They were both in the war and would sit and talk for hours."

Nurse Donaldson led Thomas down one of the halls to Room 18 and introduced him to Mr. Conetti.

"Dave, this is Thomas. He would like to talk to you about Johnny."

Thomas saw an obvious opening to break the ice.

"Mr. Conetti, I see from your cap you're a Marine vet, World War II."

Conetti snapped to attention and saluted, "Oohrah … once a Marine, always a Marine, Semper Fi."

Conetti went on to tell Thomas about his time in the military and how he had fought with some good men on Iwo Jima during World War II. Thomas thanked him for his service.

"I have some questions about John Nash. Did John ever have any visitors?"

"No, he was the nicest guy in the world, had many friends here, but no living family members. His son died a long time ago. I think it was drugs. Johnny's wife used to come by, lovely woman, but she died a year ago ... Do you mind if we talk in the dining hall? They won't be serving lunch much longer, and this Marine doesn't like to miss a meal."

Thomas and Conetti walked down the long corridor to the dining hall and found seats. Conetti plopped down next to an already seated gentleman.

"Hi Jerry, how you doing?" Conetti said to him. "This is Thomas, he's a fireman, and he's been asking questions about our friend Johnny."

Thomas extended his hand. "Hi Jerry, I'm glad to meet you."

Jerry just grunted but squeezed Thomas' hand. Jerry was well over 6 feet tall, close to 300 pounds and had a massive grip. Thomas winced, impressed with Jerry's strength at his age.

Nurse Donaldson spotted Thomas in the dining hall and came over.

"I see you met Mr. Moriarty," she said, nodding at Jerry. "Will you be joining Dave and Jerry for lunch, Tom?"

"No, thanks, but could I have some water?" Thomas felt a little shaky, not haven taken any Oxycodone yet that day. He washed down the medicine with half a bottle of water and followed it with a couple of Tums, trying to keep the stomach pain at bay.

Jerry spoke loudly. "It's a damn shame, what they did to ol' Johnny!"

Thomas was startled. "Excuse me. What *who* did to Johnny?"

Jerry explained that he had been a sheriff's deputy for Yuma County for over 25 years and that most of that time was spent as a detective.

"I guess it's just second nature for me to watch people and try to size them up." Jerry laughed. "I seem to have more time to do that nowadays."

Thomas leaned forward. "Jerry, what did you see or figure out?"

"Well, the evening them two young fellas came to pick up ol' Johnny, I was in my room. My window overlooks the parking lot. I seen that white van here before, and I was just curious, you know. Well, anyway, those two young fellas picked up Johnny and wheeled him to the van. They put the gurney in the van. Then they left the back door of the van open a smidgeon, likely 'cause it had been such a hot day. I could see pretty clearly inside. This one fella was a cutting on Johnny's chest, then they begun stuffing baggies of something into the hole they made in him. That just ain't right."

Thomas had a pretty good idea of what that might have meant, but he asked Jerry.

"What did do you think was going on?"

"Look, I didn't just fall off the turnip truck. I worked the Narcotics Task Force myself for years. The Yuma sector is a hotbed for illegal drug trafficking. Some things never change, you know. I'll bet you a dollar to a donut, them boys were stuffing ol' Johnny with drugs, but ain't nobody going to listen to an old fool like me ... Just ain't right."

"What did the fellow doing the stuffing look like?"

"He was the older of the two, maybe 5-foot-9, 180 pounds, dark hair and a small goatee, tattoo on his right arm. The younger one might have been in his teens still, same height, but closer to 135 pounds."

Those descriptions were very accurate depictions of the warehouse pick-up guys, Steve and Todd.

Thomas thanked Dave and Jerry and excused himself for the long drive home.

Thomas had his CD playing loudly before he left the parking lot of Villa Nueva. He drove all the way home listening to the Beach Boys and Jimmy Buffet tunes. The window was rolled down, a slight wind blowing desert heat across his face.

Never having such a case before, Thomas was trying to run all the scenarios through his head, trying to figure out what to do next as he sped back toward California.

Chapter 10

Drugs

Monday morning, and Thomas was in his office early to review all his reports and notes on the warehouse fire. He would call Todd Sherwood into his office for a face-to-face interview, since Thomas had new information to go on. Thomas figured Todd might be the weak link in the chain. He seemed a little uncomfortable working with the "customers" on the night of the fire.

Todd showed up at Fire Headquarters around 2:30 pm. Thomas thanked him for coming and led him to Thomas' small office, closing the door behind him.

"I'm going to record this interview for future reference, if you don't mind."

"Sure, but I don't know what I can tell you about the fire."

Thomas turned on his recorder and set it down on his desk.

"Could you state and spell your name for me?"

"Todd Sherwood, S-H-E-R-W-O-O-D."

"How old are you, Todd?"

"Nineteen"

"How long have you worked for Harold Baker?"

"About three months"

Thomas laid out what he had learned about the fire and the picking up of "customers" in Arizona.

"I'm going to read you your rights at this point: You have the right to remain silent, anything you say can and will be used against you in a court of law. If you can't afford an attorney, one will be appointed to you at no cost. Do you understand these rights as I have read them to you?"

Todd's voice cracking: "Yes."

"Knowing these rights, would you like to talk to me now?"

"Yes sir."

"Look Todd, I know you're young and maybe you didn't know what you were getting into when you took this job. If you cooperate with me perhaps the judge will take that into consideration."

Todd bowed his head, "Yes, it was horrible ... but it paid so well."

Todd went on in great detail about how Steve had cut into the bodies and stuffed bags of what he assumed to be drugs into the body cavities.

"Do you know what the drugs were?"

"No sir, they looked like pills of some sort in some baggies, and other baggies looked like white rocks in it. Some of it was just marijuana."

"How many trips did you take to Villa Nueva?"

"That was only my third trip to Arizona, but my first to that retirement home. Sometimes, we would take a customer from California, then drive to Arizona. Steve would then fill the customers with the baggies and drive back to the warehouse."

"Where did you and Steve get the drugs?"

"Steve would get a text from someone, telling him what time to go to the pick-up spot."

"Do you know who texted him?"

"No sir."

"Where was the pick-up spot?"

"Steve drove to a dirt road off East County 14th Street near Somerton. Under a large bush was a small locker buried in the sand.

Steve would get whatever was in the locker, put a stack of money in it, then bury the locker in sand again."

"What was the procedure then, once Steve had the drugs?"

"Well, on that day, he drove to that place, Villa Nueva, to pick up a customer. We wheeled the customer to the van, then Steve cut a hole in the body, and he stuffed the baggies down into the body ... I almost threw-up the first time I seen it. But all I did was hand him the baggies, he did the cutting and stuffing. Then Steve would sew up the hole again before we headed back to California."

Thomas asked a few more questions, then ended the interview. "Do you understand this conversation was recorded?"

"Yes sir."

"I'm going to end the recording now."

Thomas shut off the recorder. "Todd, I don't think you wanted any of this to happen. You just got caught up in it. I'm going to let you go home. Don't tell anyone, and find any excuse you can to not go back to Arizona. I'll see what I can do for you with the District Attorney if you continue to help me, and ... don't tell anyone!"

"Yes, sir! Thank you so much. I'm just glad it's over."

"One more question. Why did you do it?"

"Steve paid me real well, sir, and another thing ... Steve is my cousin, he got me this job. I didn't want to let him down."

"You can't tell anyone you were here. Especially Steve!"

Chapter II

Reinforcements

On Tuesday morning, Thomas walked through the kitchen of Station 1 and poured himself a cup of strong coffee, as he had every other morning. He thought the Evergreen warehouse fire was way beyond anything Captain Thompson had ever encountered, and Thomas didn't want the captain to know about the trip to Arizona. Not just yet, anyway.

The only thing Thomas could think to do was to call Henry Romero, a friend he made while attending one of his classes. Henry worked for Alcohol, Tobacco and Firearms (ATF), out of the Glendale field office. Henry had greater experience in fire investigation than anyone Thomas knew.

"Hey Hank, this is Tom. I need to sound some stuff off you regarding a case I'm working." Thomas then proceeded to lay out the main points of the case.

Investigator Romero interrupted him. "You know, I have an interview out your way this morning. How about I come by after lunch?"

"That sounds great, I look forward to seeing you again."

Thomas spent the rest of the morning going over all the incident reports from the last weekend, finding nothing of any interest or in need of follow-up. He pored over the photos and reports from the Evergreen warehouse fire again.

At 1:30, Agent Henry Romero showed up, and he had a woman with him whom Thomas did not recognize.

"Tom, this is Nicole Mitchell with the Drug Enforcement Agency, Los Angeles office. I've worked with her on a couple of my cases. After hearing your story, I thought we might want to get them involved."

"Well … OK … I think it may be time I pulled Captain Thompson back in on this one, then. I don't want to step on any more toes than I already may have."

Thomas paged Captain Thompson to the conference room, where Henry and the DEA agent were already waiting.

"I sorry to spring this on you, Captain Thompson, but I've learned some disturbing stuff about the Evergreen warehouse fire and thought we could use some help." Thomas took a swig of water and a Tums before he made introductions.

He explained what he had learned to that point and how he thought Steve and Todd had been smuggling drugs into California and that the fire might have been set in a turf war over drug sales.

Agent Mitchell addressed the group regarding the Yuma sector being very active in drug trafficking, and that she was aware that drug activity was acutely high in Southern California at the time. They just didn't have a handle on where it had been coming from.

"I'll take this back to our Senior Agent and get back with you on a course of action," Agent Mitchell concluded.

Thomas then handed her copies of all the reports he had generated on the case to that point.

Everyone left the conference room except Captain Thompson and Thomas. The captain didn't look happy.

"Don't leave, Tom," he said. "I need to talk with you."

Thomas sat down again after taking another gulp of water. "I know, captain, I know."

"Tom, you're in way over your head. We are FIRE INVESTIGATORS! Not narcs! The chief will have your hide if he finds you following this any further."

"Yeah, that's why I asked for help. Sorry I didn't fill you in sooner, captain."

Thomas turned to leave the room when Captain Thompson spoke again.

"Thomas … unofficially ... good job."

"Thanks, captain."

Later that afternoon, Thomas left for a scheduled doctor's appointment for updates on his progress and to get a new script for Oxycodone. Thomas ran out of refills, and had gone without the medicine Sunday afternoon.

Thomas felt weak and was shaking a little without his medication. He sat quietly in the doctor's office, and placed his hands on his lap to hide the shaking. It didn't work. The trembling was obvious to the doctor.

"I'm very concerned that you're still reporting pain a year after the surgery, Tom. That should have stopped months ago."

The doctor reminded Thomas about the dangers of long-term use of Oxycodone. He then gave Thomas the prescription he had asked for.

"I'm going to taper off the dose to get you free of the pain meds," he said. "If you still have pain after this, we'll have to address it differently."

Thomas felt relieved and panicked at the same time. Filling the prescription, he took one right away and chased it by chewing a Tums and downing a bottle of water.

Thomas struggled all week with the new dose of Oxycodone and knew he would run out early if he couldn't pace the dose.

Feeling a little lonely and, trying to keep his family off his mind, he decided to try his hand at surfing again. He hadn't been surfing since before he had injured his back and lost his wife and kids in that tragic accident.

Early Wednesday morning, Thomas loaded his board in the bed of his old truck and headed out for the beach. He actually felt pretty good for a guy with a couple of rods and six screws in his back.

      After an hour, Thomas headed to the station feeling tired but exhilarated from being on the waves again and feeling the wind and salt air again. Thomas was anxious to see what plan Agent Thompson and the DEA had come up with.

Chapter 12

The Deal

It was Wednesday afternoon when the phone in Thomas' office rang. "Fire Investigations, Investigator Cheshire."

"Investigator Cheshire, this is DEA Agent Mitchell, we met at your station last week?"

"Yes, Nicole, you can call me Tom."

"Tom, we've come up with an action plan. We took your reports to the U.S. Attorney's office, and they're willing to not press charges on your witness, Sherwood, in exchange for cooperation that leads to the arrest and conviction of Stephen Douglas and anyone else involved, in what looks to be a drug cartel operation."

"Great, the kid doesn't seem the type. I think he'll be helpful. I know he'll go for it."

"Arrange a meeting with your witness, and I'll lay out the plan for you."

"I'll set it up for tomorrow in the morning if I can."

Thomas contacted Todd Sherwood and asked him to come by the station.

It was a Thursday morning when Agent Mitchell and Thomas met in the fire station conference room and sat down with Todd.

Agent Mitchell spoke first and read Todd his rights.

"Todd, you face some very serious charges, but the U.S. Department of Justice is willing to cut you some slack in return for your cooperation."

"Yes, ma'am! Anything!"

"Do you know who has been contacting your partner, Steve, regarding the drugs?"

"No ma'am."

"Do you know who is placing the drugs in the desert locker for you to pick up?"

"No ma'am!"

"Do you know who's distributing the drugs once they're brought back to California?"

"No ma'am!"

"OK, if you want to get out of the mess you're in, we'll need your cooperation on your next trip to Arizona."

"Yes ma'am! But Investigator Cheshire told me not to go to Arizona."

"Well, in order for you to get out of trouble, we'll need you to make one last trip. When you're headed to Arizona again, I want you to text this number." Agent Mitchell slid a piece of paper across the table. "At that point, your job is pretty much done. Just take the ride like you have in the past. Understand?"

"Yes, ma'am."

"Do not tell anyone you were here today, or what we talked about, or your deal is off."

"Yes, ma'am."

Thomas added, "Todd, I understand that on the night of the fire, another vehicle was in the parking lot with the white van. Did you and Steve have separate vehicles, or was someone else in the area?"

"No, just Steve and I. The other vehicle may have been Mr. Baker's."

Todd was told he could go, and he rushed out the door after a long sigh.

Thomas asked the DEA agent what the next move was going to be.

"The text number I gave Todd is to our Phoenix Division," she said. "They've been filled in already and have copies of all your reports and will get the one that I generate today. Once they get the text, they'll send teams to the desert location to intercede. We already have aerial surveillance of the area. If someone makes a drop, our Yuma people will be on top of them before they even know we're in the area."

"You know I've been in on this from the beginning," Thomas said, "and I still have a fire I need to find an arsonist for. Could you keep me in the loop?"

"Certainly, your contact will be Senior Agent Brett Webb. I'll have him contact you once the van is on the move." Nicole jotted something down on the back of her business card and slid it across the table. "Here's his direct number so that you can introduce yourself."

Agent Mitchell left, and Thomas set out to re-read his reports yet again. When he got to the phone interview of Mr. Baker, he noticed that he had claimed he was out of town on the night of the fire, but Todd had said that Baker's car was at the warehouse on the night of the fire.

Thomas immediately drove to Baker's home to interview him in person. Baker stood about 5-foot-10, with a slim build and dark hair, and he appeared to be in his mid-40's. Judging from the photos in the living room, Baker was married and had two young daughters. Thomas also noted a photo of Steve Douglas, Baker's stepson.

An average family, living the American dream, Thomas thought. He confronted Baker.

"Your employees stated that they saw you in the building on the night of the fire."

Baker paused, then said, "What day was the fire again?"

"It was Saturday, the 23rd, a little after midnight."

"Oh, oh, yes, Saturday … I was confused on the date of the fire. I was in the warehouse doing an embalming procedure."

"Do you remember seeing Steve or Todd in the building that night?"

"I do not."

When the interview concluded, Baker got up to escort Thomas to the door. Thomas noted that Baker had a Smith and Wesson Model 60, snub-nose, hand gun holstered on his right hip. Remembering that Baker had said that he had a conceal carry permit, Thomas let it go.

Thomas returned to the station and made the introductory call to Agent Webb, who expressed his gratitude for the lead.

"Thank you so much, Investigator Cheshire. This could be big for us."

"No problem. Call me Tom. Look, Agent Webb ... Brett ... I'm still trying to solve an arson back here. Could you let me know when things start to go down? You know, so I can tie up loose ends here?"

"Absolutely, give me your cell number and you'll get my call."

Thomas wrote up the latest interview with Baker before going home for the night.

Friday morning came, and Thomas didn't have to wait long for his call from Agent Brett Webb. It came that afternoon.

"Tom, I just got a text from your informant," Webb said. "They'll be heading out this way in the morning."

Webb gave Thomas directions to where he could meet up with his team. "Text me when you get into town."

Thomas made a beeline to Captain Thompson's office and, without filling him in, Thomas asked for the rest of afternoon off on comp time.

"Sure Tom," the captain said. "Got big plans for the weekend?"

"Yeah, I'm going to the river to water ski, and I just want to get ready."

"Sure, I'll mark you off. Have a great time, you deserve it."

Chapter 13

Arizona Bound

Thomas rushed home and packed his bag, also taking a few bottles of water, his Oxycodone and Tums for the overnight trip, and dashed out the door. He wanted to beat the weekend traffic.

Thomas' CDs of the Beach Boys and Jimmy Buffet kept him company again as he drove along the Southern California coast and then headed east across the desert.

The air was still but very warm by the time he reached the Arizona border. It was close to 6 p.m. when Thomas pulled into the El Rancho Motel in Yuma. It was nothing fancy, a single-story road motel, but it did have a pool that Thomas thought he might enjoy later if it didn't cool down soon.

Thomas checked into his room and tossed his bag on the bed. He sent a text message to Agent Webb before unpacking: "At the Yuma, El Rancho Motel."

Agent Webb returned a text: "Meet me at Brewer's Restaurant & Sports Bar. I'll be wearing a blue windbreaker."

Thomas made his way over to the restaurant and quickly found Agent Webb already seated by himself. Thomas introduced himself and sat across the table from him. Thomas ordered a hamburger and a glass of beer before Agent Webb spoke.

"We've had some action on the case since I spoke with you last," Webb said. "Earlier today, our surveillance team spotted a vehicle on the dirt road off of East County 14th Street. Didn't think much about until he stopped next to a large bush. He then proceeded to put a few packages down and pushed dirt over them again."

"Great! Good work, Brett."

"Well, here's the thing … The vehicle was a border agent's truck."

"What! You gotta be kidding me!"

"I wish I were, but he's not the first." Webb shook his head. "We know the vehicle number and have good photos of the agent. We didn't pick him up, in case he's the one working with your pick-up guys. It looks like our border agent may be working with the drug cartel and handing off the stuff to your guys, who in turn sell it on the streets of L.A. I'll have aerial surveillance on the white van after it leaves California. Stay close to your phone until you hear from me."

"All right. I'll see you tomorrow, Brett."

The agent stood and walked out. Thomas finished his dinner, then retreated to his motel room. The night air was still and warm from the ground that was reflecting heat it had absorbed during the day. Thomas changed into his trunks and took a swim in the pool. He was trying to relax from the long drive and the building tension of what the DEA agent was now calling the "Evergreen Case."

Thomas watched a few minutes of the news, took an Oxycodone, washed it down with a bottle of water and drifted off to sleep.

Despite the Oxycodone, Thomas tossed and turned, waking several times, his mind burning through developments in the Evergreen Case. He got up early, anxious about what was about to go down. He ate a quick breakfast and went back to his room to await the phone call from Agent Webb.

Back in California, Steve Douglas and Todd Sherwood drove to a hospital in Pasadena and loaded a body into their refrigerated van in preparation for the trip to Arizona. No one would question the employees transporting a body for cremation. Steve had made this drive many times, but for Todd, this was still new.

Todd was nervous during the long drive to Arizona. Though he didn't know what was going to happen or when it would happen, he was sure something would disrupt the trip today.

The white van approached the California/Arizona border checkpoint, which was routinely manned by the Department of Food and Agriculture. Cars were being stopped and questioned about transport of fruits and vegetables coming from Arizona into California, but they had no such check point coming from California to Arizona. On this day, a Highway Patrol officer was at the border, observing every vehicle entering Arizona.

The white van passed into Arizona, and the officer called Agent Webb.

"They're headed your way," the officer said.

"Thanks. We'll take it from here. I'll get a drone up and follow them now."

Chapter 14

Go Time

Thomas' phone rang at a little after 1 p.m.

"Tom, it's Derek from the DEA's office. Saddle up and head to the command post. They're getting close, and I want to brief you."

Thomas swallowed hard and said, "I'll be right over."

He rushed to his truck, threw his bag onto the passenger seat, and drove down to Yuma International Airport. Thomas then walked down toward the south end of the runway, where the command post was set up. Thomas met up with Derek, who had a couple of other DEA agents in unmarked cars with him.

"Tom, a lot has happened," Derek said. "We were able to identify the Border Agent as Manny Hernandez. He's been an agent for six years, mostly in this sector. He's on duty again today. We have surveillance on him, too."

Agent Webb explained that he had developed other information from a suspect already in custody.

"MS-13 gang members have been tossing the drugs over the border fence," Webb said. "Agent Hernandez would then pick up the drugs while on patrol and place them in a locker at the pickup spot. Hernandez would then text your guys in the van to pick-up the drugs. Apparently, Hernandez has been bought by MS-13. We believe the trail goes from MS-13 to Agent Hernandez to Steve and Todd, who distribute them to MS-13 members in the Los Angeles area."

Thomas was intrigued by the information, but he had another mystery on his mind.

"Any clues on my arson case?" he asked.

"I believe that MS-13 may have been disrupting drug sales of either the Bloods or the Crips," Webb said. "Perhaps they stole the drugs from the Evergreen location and then set the fire to cover-up the crime. Today's bust will be good for us and should put a big dent in the drug flow. I'm sure you'll find your arsonist before we're done."

Fifteen more minutes passed, and Thomas spotted the white van. "There she is."

Agent Webb spoke into his radio: "On my word, go."
The white van pulled off East County 14th Street and headed south onto a dirt road. It pulled to a stop adjacent to where the buried locker was located. The informant, Todd Sherwood, was behind the wheel. Steve Douglas slid out of the passenger seat and walked over to the buried locker. Just as Steve unearthed the locker, Agent Webb gave the word: "GO!"

Agent vehicles entered the dirt road from south and the north, sliding to a stop in front of, and behind, the van. Agents poured out with guns drawn. Todd and a very-shocked Steve were unarmed and surrendered immediately. The two were cuffed and placed into separate vehicles.

Thomas leaned into the government car where Todd had been placed and whispered, "It's going to be OK," then gave Todd a little wink.

Ten baggies of methamphetamines and eight baggies of crack cocaine were recovered from the now-open locker. The feds also recovered a note that read: "Last drop until we get what is owed."

At that exact time, at another location close to the border, border agent Hernandez was being pulled over by Drug Enforcement Agents. Hernandez was disarmed and taken into custody without incident.

Agents transported Hernandez and Steve Douglas to the Yuma Detention Center for booking and questioning. Todd Sherwood was un-cuffed after his cousin, Steve Douglas, had cleared the scene. Steve had no idea that it had been Todd who turned on him, bringing the operation to a close.

After questioning, Todd was released, thanked for his cooperation and told that he would need to testify in court.

Thomas offered to give Todd a ride back to California while Drug Enforcement Agents tried to figure out what to do with the van with a corpse in it.

Thomas set out to make the long trip back to California with Todd in the passenger seat. After several miles of uncomfortable silence, Thomas tried to make small talk.

"Do you like sports?"

"Yeah, baseball ... I like the Dodgers."

"I do, too. I played pro ball for a short time with the Mariners organization." Thomas went on about how he played for a couple of seasons but got hurt, and about how he came to be a firefighter.

Thomas had built up a trust, and Todd began to feel at ease. The conversation came around to Todd's family.

Todd said Steve was his aunt Cynthia's son from a previous marriage, and she had married Harold Baker about 10 years ago. Steve's aunt and Baker had two daughters of their own.

Small talk trailed off, and Thomas started to gently press Todd.

"Do you know what Steve did with the drugs once he got them back to the Evergreen warehouse?"

"No ... I'm really just the pick-up guy, to help Steve move bodies from one location to another. I was shocked the first time I saw him cut into a body."

"Did Steve contact or hang around guys that may have been gang members?"

"I really don't know. Steve and I were never very close until he needed help moving customers."

Todd gave Thomas directions to where his vehicle was parked. Thomas dropped Todd off near a warehouse at the outskirts of Los Angeles. Todd told Thomas that this was the new location of Baker's warehouse.

Todd paused, not wanting to get out of the truck. "What am I going to do now?"

"Look, Todd, you're going to be OK. Just don't tell anyone what happened, and don't answer any phone calls from Mr. Baker until I can figure this out."

Monday morning came, and Thomas was anxious and ready to get to the station to work on the Evergreen case. He walked into his office and checked the calendar. Thomas noted that the "C" shift was on duty. He knew he needed to see someone at Station 2 before he did anything else.

Thomas slid into his department sedan and drove to Station 2. Thomas walked past Engine 2 and a couple of the firefighters without saying a word. He walked into the captain's office and found Captain Osborne alone, sitting at his desk.

"Captain … Derek. Can I talk with you this morning, as our chaplain, not as a captain? I have something I need to talk about."

"OK, I was about to get a cup of coffee. Why don't you grab one, too, and we'll come back here and talk."

The men got their cups and came back into the office. Chaplain Osborne closed and locked the door behind him. He gave Thomas a small smile.

"I was wondering when you were going to come see me."

"Is it that obvious?"

"It has been to me for a while now. I went through the same thing with a back problem I had before you hired on. It's a process, it's tough to get through, but the department won't look down on you as long as you get the help you need."

"Why didn't you? … why didn't you …?"

"Why didn't I say anything to you? To be helped, you have to want help. No one can make you. The important thing is that you're here now."

Chaplain Osborne gave advice to Thomas about death, survivors' guilt and addiction.

"It's not your fault," he said.

After several minutes, Thomas began to cry. The loss of his family and the addiction all caught up with him. He was finally grieving his loss and facing his own demons.

Chaplain Osborn went on to explain that the treatment involved 30 days in-patient care with follow-up, and that the department would back him all the way.

"The pain medicine was because of your job-related injury, so the treatment will also be handled as job-related. I can arrange to have you admitted today, Tom."

"Thank you so much for your time and advice. It's invaluable." Thomas pulled a tissue out of the box on Osborn's desk and dried his eyes. "I'll think about it, while I tie up some loose ends."

"OK, Tom, but don't wait too long. I hope you know what you're doing, If you let this opportunity go, the department may not back you."

"Thank you."

"I'm serious. Don't wait too long. You can stay in my office as long as it takes to compose yourself."

Captain Osborne walked out of the office, shutting the door behind him. Thomas sat, lost in thought for a while, then took a last sip of coffee and drove back to his Headquarters office to do more follow-up on the Evergreen case.

Chapter 15

Arsonist Identified

Thomas rushed into the station kitchen and poured himself a fresh cup of coffee without speaking to anyone. He then made a beeline to Captain Thompson's office.

The captain had just sat down with his own cup of coffee when Thomas started laying out what had happened over the weekend. Thomas intentionally left out the part where he was actually in Arizona when the takedowns occurred.

"Captain, I have a theory in regard to who set the fire. Members of a gang may have done it over a drug war. I just don't know how I'm going to figure out which gang may be involved."

"Well, let's try to eliminate Mr. Baker as a suspect first. We don't know if Baker was involved in the drugs or if it ended with his stepson."

"Yes, he did appear to be less than truthful in my interviews, and he had opportunity. I just can't figure out what his motive might be."

"Well, good work, keep following it and keep me updated."

Thomas retreated to his office to write follow-up reports. At his desk, he felt a little weak and shaky because of the lower dose of Oxycodone he had been taking. Thomas was only a couple of sentences into the follow-up report when his phone rang.

"Tom, it's Brett from the Yuma Sector DEA office."

"Yeah, what's up Brett?"

"The passenger, Steve Douglas, sang like a bird once we had him in lockup. Looks like the owner is in this thing up to his eyeballs."

Agent Webb went on to tell Thomas that the owner, Harold Baker, was the one who set up the transportation of drugs from the Yuma area to California in body cavities. He told them that Border Agent Hernandez had been a high school buddy, and that the two of them were partners in the plan. Baker would then sell the drugs to dealers in the Los Angeles area.

Apparently, Baker had a gambling and drug problem himself and got behind on his payments to Border Agent Hernandez, who in turn fell behind to MS-13. When Drug Enforcement Agents checked Steven Douglas' phone, they saw a text from Hernandez that said that this would be the last delivery until he paid what was due.

"Steve told us that Baker's drug and gambling problem had been a big issue with Steve's mom," Webb said, "and that she had moved out on him a few weeks ago, taking the girls with her. I don't know if MS-13 burned him because he fell behind, if his wife did it, or if he did it himself. Thought you would want to know."

"Thanks, Brett. Could you email me that information? I may need it for my reports."

"Yeah, no problem. Some of it will be redacted, but you'll get them."

Thomas went back to Captain Thompson to bring him up to speed. The captain, standing and staring out a window, thought for a moment, then spoke.

"Tom, contact the owner's insurance company and see what his coverage was. That may give us the motive. He appears to have had a cash flow problem."

"Great idea, I'm on it."

Thomas had learned, from previous interviews, that the warehouse had been insured by the Tushman Insurance Group.

Thomas called and was able to talk with the adjuster. Thomas learned that not only was Baker well insured, but that he had increased his insurance just two weeks prior to the loss. Thomas now had what he needed for an arrest warrant; means, motive and opportunity.

Thomas set out writing an arrest warrant. By the time Thomas was done, it was too close to 5 p.m. to file it, so he would have to wait until morning.

Tuesday morning, Thomas gathered all his reports and supporting reports from the Drug Enforcement Agents, then headed down to the District Attorney's Office. The case to file an arson arrest warrant was an easy sell to the District Attorney, and an even easier sell to the judge who signed the warrant.

Thomas was leaving the courthouse when he got a call on his cell phone.

"Hello"

"Tom, it's Nicole, Los Angeles DEA Office."

"Yes, Nicole, what can I do for you?"

"I'm just giving you a heads-up since it's about a case you're working. We are getting ready to arrest Harold Baker on drug trafficking charges. It will likely go down today."

"Nicole, I have a warrant on him in my hand for the arson. I was just on my way to arrest him."

"OK, I'll tell you what, if you can wait until 3 this afternoon, we can do this together. He'll go down on both charges."

Chapter 16

Takedown

Thomas arranged to meet in the parking lot of a Denny's restaurant near the new warehouse location in Los Angeles so that they could jointly arrest Baker. Thomas arrived first, Agent Mitchell pulling in just a couple of minutes behind him. Agent Mitchell had brought her partner, Agent Marty Newcomb, to assist in the arrest.

Thomas and the two Drug Enforcement Agents caravanned to the new warehouse location but found the business locked up. Thomas and the agents checked the neighboring business and found that the only activity seen lately was from a white van a few days prior.

Thomas and the agents then caravanned over to Harold Baker's home to see if they could apprehend him there. Thomas and the agents were sure that Baker must be fully aware by now that Steven, Todd and Border Agent Hernandez had been arrested, and that authorities would be coming for him soon.

Agent Newcomb quietly made his way around to the backdoor of the residence, while Thomas and Agent Mitchell went to the front door. Thomas knocked loudly on the front door. The tension Thomas felt was broken when he heard: "Bang! Bang!" The sounds of two gunshots.

The rounds splintered wood as they passed through the front door. The first round also passed through Thomas' left, upper arm like a hot poker iron. Thomas staggered backward and fell over the porch railing and into a flower bed below.

Agent Mitchell instantly drew her gun, pointing toward the door as she retreated. Agent Newcomb ran from his position in the backyard, and grabbed Thomas as the three of them retreated to the cover of their vehicles.

Thomas' left arm dangled limply by his side, broken and bleeding. He grabbed his portable radio from his hip.

"Dispatch, this is Investigator Two. We have shots fired, and I've been hit. We have a barricaded felony suspect. Dispatch medical aid and police for back-up."

"Ten-four, Investigator Two ... address?"

"7748 Duncan Lane."

Thomas and the two agents were watching the dwelling to see if anyone tried to exit when they heard "Bang! Bang!" as two more rounds went off from inside the dwelling.

Another minute passed before dark smoke appeared along one side of the dwelling. Sirens could now be heard in the distance, as police and Medic 2 approached.

Thomas thought back to the interview he had with Baker. He remembered that Baker had been carrying a Smith and Wesson Model 60. A weapon that carried five rounds.

Thomas grabbed his portable radio again, "Dispatch, Investigator two, send me a first alarm. We now have a structure fire at this location." As he finished, another gunshot came from inside the building. Thomas said out loud, "Five ... that's five shots."

After a few seconds passed, dispatch could be heard over the radio, "Engine 2, Engine 1, Truck 1, Medic 2, BC 1; structure fire 7748 Duncan Lane. Stage until PD clears the scene ... shots fired."

Thomas was sweating profusely and felt weak as blood ran down his arm. Gathering all the strength he could, he dashed from the safety of his vehicle and ran toward the back of the dwelling.

The Drug Enforcement Agents yelled for him to stop as he disappeared behind the dwelling. Thomas had a pretty good idea of the layout of the dwelling, since he was inside it just a few days prior, while interviewing Baker.

The fire had progressed quickly, and flames were coming through a couple of windows when Thomas reached a sliding glass door. Looking in, he saw two young girls lying on the floor just inside the door. They were lying in a pool of blood, but moving, as smoke was starting to bank down.

Holding his breath, Thomas slid the door open and made his way to the first girl. She had an obvious wound to her abdomen, but was moaning and moving her legs. Thomas grabbed her wrist with his right hand and dragged her through the room, out the door and into the backyard. Thomas then held his breath again and re-entered the dwelling. He found the smoke was much heavier by now, and had banked down to within two feet of floor level.

Thomas found the second, younger, girl, a little deeper into the room. She was struggling to get to her feet by the time he reached her. Thomas held her with his good arm, supporting her as she limped into the backyard. Once outside, he could see clearly that her wound had been to her upper leg. Thomas quickly instructed her how to hold pressure over the wound to slow down the bleeding.

Holding his breath again, Thomas entered the dwelling a third time, passing through the family room and toward the front of the dwelling. The room was well involved in fire, the heat and smoke intense. Thomas could no longer hold his breath and had to retreat outside.

Captain Osborne and his crew laid out hose lines from a safe distance, for exposure protection. Drug Enforcement Agent Mitchell flagged Captain Osborne down as he was giving orders to his crew. "One of your guys, Tom, is in the back, I think he went inside."

Captain Osborne immediately redirected his crew to the back of the dwelling. When they got there with their hose line, they found Thomas kneeling over the older girl, trying to stop the bleeding from her abdomen. Thomas' arm hung by his side, limp and still bleeding.

Captain Osborne approached Thomas.

"Tom, are you OK?"

"I'm hit in the arm, I'm sure it's broken ... I don't think we're in danger any more. We heard the last shot right after the fire started ... Derek, you've got a couple of live ones, please save them."

The dwelling was well-involved in fire at that point. Flames were through the roof, and a column of dark smoke rose high in the air. No one could be in the building and still be alive. Captain Osborne instructed his crew to begin interior fire attack while the other incoming units were starting to protect the exposures.

Medic 2 and a private ambulance company attended to the two young girls. Both girls were transported to Harbor General Hospital with serious but non-life-threatening injuries.

Firefighters ushered Thomas back to the front of the dwelling, where Medic 1 was waiting to bandage and sling his wounded arm. Medics started an IV and placed him on the gurney. Thomas was wheeled toward an ambulance when he stopped the medics.

"Please get Captain Osborne, I need to speak with him before we go."

The fire, while not yet extinguished, was under control. Captain Osborne walked back to the rear of the ambulance.

"You OK, Tom? What do you need?"

"Yeah, it takes more than this to put me down. You know that." Thomas reached into the pocket of this wind breaker jacket to grab something. "Chaplain ... Derek ... I'm done." Thomas then reached for Captain Osborne's hand, opened it, pushed the vial of Oxycodone into his hands, and closed the captain's fingers around it. "I'm ready for your help."

"I called them right after you saw me in the office. They're saving a bed for you. Get well, and get back here quick, Tom."

The Drug Enforcement Agency could close their book on Baker. His body had been found in the master bedroom. He had to be identified with dental records, as he had been burned beyond recognition.

His surviving daughters told police officers that their mom had dropped them off for visitation earlier in the day. Their dad had shot them when someone knocked on the front door.

Baker apparently could not deal with his debt, his family leaving him, his addictions and his impending legal problems. The body was found on top of his Smith and Wesson, Model 60. All five rounds expended. A charred gas can was found near by. His autopsy revealed that he had methamphetamine in his system and that he had died of a single, self inflicted gunshot to the head.

Thomas, too, could close his books on Baker and the Evergreen Case. It was obvious that Baker had set the Evergreen warehouse on fire to collect insurance money, in order to pay off his debt to the drug traffickers. Thomas also theorized that John Nash's body was dumped in the middle of the warehouse to make it look like gang members had messed up the place before setting it on fire. However, it would be close to six weeks before Thomas would get back to work to close his report with this information.

Thanks to the cooperation of Todd Sherwood and another, unidentified witness from the Yuma Detention Center, Steve Douglas would stand trial for drug trafficking and desecration of a corpse. Border Patrol Agent Hernandez was also charged for his part in trafficking drugs. Sentencing for such crimes was five to 40 years in Federal prison. The MS-13 drug traffickers, however, remained at large in Mexico and in the United States and continued to be a problem.

Investigator Thomas Cheshire would heal from the arm injury which had to be repaired with a plate and screws. Thomas rehabbed in the hospital for a couple of days, then was admitted to a treatment center while his arm healed and he recovered from his drug addiction. Thomas spent 30 days in the center while he went through withdrawal and counseling. He used his free time to study for a promotional exam.

Thomas was assigned to a counselor upon his release. Thomas left the treatment center to become a happy and healthy member of his fire department once again, and continued to investigate fires.

Chapter 17
Epilogue

Home Again

Thomas, released from treatment, returned to Headquarters Station to speak with the chief. Thomas had found that while he was in rehab, Chief Clayborne retired and Battalion Chief Raymond Mendoza had been appointed to take his place. This was a great relief to Thomas, because Chief Mendoza supported Thomas and was a big supporter of the Fire Investigation program.

"Sit down, Tom," Chief Mendoza said. "How does it feel to be back here?"

"Great! I was just in the kitchen visiting with the other firefighters. Feels like home again."

"Well, it's good to have you back … and by that, I mean all the way back."

"Thank you, sir."

"I want you to know that you have been nominated for a medal of valor for your actions leading to saving the lives of the two Baker girls. Their mother has been by a couple of times, wanting to thank you in person. I told her you would be in today."

"Is she the one who nominated me sir?"

"No, I did … now get back to work, before I tear up."

"Yes, sir! Thank you sir!"

Thomas was back at his old job, but it felt different. He had made peace and accepted the fact that his wife and children had passed. He would always have their memory. He was in a happier place now. He quickly closed out the paperwork on the Evergreen warehouse fire. Within a week, Thomas had taken a promotional examination and placed well on the list.

A couple of months passed before Chief Mendoza called Thomas back into his office.

"Tom, I have two captain spots opening up. Captain Osborne is retiring out of Station 2, and Captain Thompson is retiring out of the Fire Investigation Unit. Both slots open at the end of the month. You're next up on the list. The choice is yours. Do you want to go back to an engine company, or do you want stay on as head of the Investigation Unit?"

"I loved working shifts at the stations, and I love working with the guys, but I think I'm best suited for fire investigations, sir. It's my home now. I would be honored to take Captain Thompson's spot."

"That's the answer I was looking for Captain Cheshire."

Drug abuse, of both prescription and illegal street drugs, is a major problem in the United States. If you or someone you know is fighting addiction, please seek help. Call 1-800-662-HELP (4357) or visit www.samhsa.gov.

Part II

Holding the Line

The next two sections are non-fiction and are from my own personal accounts, leading to becoming a firefighter, and events during my career, as I remember them. The names of people, companies and departments have been changed or omitted for privacy reasons.

Chapter 18

The Army Comes Calling

We start here, because without having being in the military, I may never have thought about the joining a paramilitary organization like the fire department.

In October of 1970, my draft notice arrived in the mail. The Vietnam War was not popular by that time, and many young men were fleeing to Canada to escape the draft. I was confused, being a very patriotic 20-year-old, but not keen on that war. I was directed to visit a counselor, who eventually recommended that I flee to Canada to avoid the draft. My mom was dead-set against me going to war, but my father, being raised by a career military man, said, "By God, one of my sons is going into the military."

I was as torn as my parents were at that point. I thought I would let it play out. Since I was an American, I believed in our Democratic Republic, and my American government wanted me to serve. However, I considered it a poorly run war effort to that point, with no clear objective.

First came the trip to the induction center, as ordered. I was put through a few tests during the day. A doctor asked a group of us if we had any reason to believe that we should not serve. A few young men gave some excuses that seemed lame, even to me. None of the excuses were accepted. When it came time for me to speak, I told the doctor that I had epilepsy. Sounding skeptical, he asked, "What medicine do you take?"

"Dilantin"

The doctor turned to address the group and said, "Now that's a reason not to serve."

I was thinking I might be one lucky young man. It was getting late in the day, and the group was excused with instructions to return the next day.

I thought I was in the clear. I had a problem with light sensitivity that would keep me out of the Army. I returned the next day. My fiancé, Debbie, dropped me off at the induction center. The understanding was that I would call her to pick me up when they excused me from service.

I was run through a lot more physical tests, the whole time thinking they would be sending me home. The group of young men I was in was led downstairs and told to line up. A couple of names were read off, and they were told that they had been drafted into the Marines (I didn't even know they could do that). The rest of us were told to raise our right hands and take the oath of service. We were herded onto a bus, and off to Fort Ord, California, we went.

At Fort Ord, we were ushered into the barber shop, where we took turns having our heads shaved to achieve the military boot look. Next we were marched through buildings, where we were given a duffle bag and all the ill-fitting uniforms we would need the next couple of years. Finally, the group was marched to our platoon barracks and told to line up in front of the building with our duffels at our feet.

The drill sergeant, a stocky young man with a very short hair cut and neatly trimmed mustache, stood before us. His uniform was neatly pressed and heavily starched, his campaign hat pulled down just above his eyes. The sergeant loudly read off four names: Leonard (South Central Los Angeles), Dave (Albuquerque), Roger (Chicago) and myself (Los Angeles suburb).

I remember thinking, "This is it, they made a mistake, and they are sending the four of us home."

The young sergeant barked out, "You four maggots are on KP duty, report to the mess hall."

The rest of the group was ordered to grab their duffles and report to the third floor as fast as they could. I later found out that the guy who was later named our platoon leader was the guy who made it to the top floor the fastest. This guy looked like Marcus Allen of the NFL Raiders and ran the stairs with reckless abandon, much like Marshawn Lynch would much later for the Seahawks. He was pushing guys left and right as he made it to the top floor, his duffle knocking people down as he passed them.

While the four of us were on KP duty, the rest of the platoon was being yelled at by the drill sergeant. The recruits were assigned bunks and instructed how to make it up so tight that a quarter could bounce off it.

Meanwhile, I was given a butter knife and told that I had to peel the largest bag of potatoes I had ever seen. I got the job done, but those potatoes were a lot smaller than they could have been if I had real peeler. It was about this time I decided to stop taking my dilantin. I figured either I had outgrown the light problem or I was going to have my first seizure and exit the Army.

After supper and clean up, the four of us on KP duty found our duffles still on the blacktop in front of the barracks. We grabbed the bags and made our way upstairs. We found that all of the bunks in the dorm were spoken for. By then, the drill instructors had left or gone to their barracks, so we went to the watch commander, who was likely a corporal. He decided the only beds left were in a room down the hall from the larger dorm. It had two bunk beds, four footlockers and four stand-up lockers in it. Being on KP that first night was going to be a Godsend for us later.

Leonard was a black fellow, about my size, who seemed to laugh a lot. Dave was also black, thin and tall, but on the more serious side. Roger was white, over six feet tall, and had a smile that

I'm sure more than one girl back home would miss. We were all roommates now.

The guy that our drill sergeant had made the platoon leader went AWOL before morning, and by morning, I mean 0400 hours (4 a.m.).

The first order of business on the first morning was to be marched over to a medical facility. We stood single-file and took our turns at getting vaccines. This was not a single shot in the arm, mind you, but something far more sinister.

Two medical people were standing at the head of the line, dressed in white lab coats. Each had some sort of pneumatic gun in their hands. When I got to the head of the line, the contraptions were placed at both shoulders, and the triggers were pushed simultaneously. "Whoosh, whoosh," and they were done. I had been hit with five different vaccines in each arm. Blood trailed down my arms from the injection sites. The rest of the day was used to practice marching, as no one could raise their arms above their heads due to the pain.

I wasn't in bad shape, having played high school football just a couple years earlier and not being overweight, at less than 140 pounds at the time. I remember words that my future brother-in-law had told me: "They can't kill you, and it's only two months long."

Our drill instructor was a mean SOB, and during the marches, if something didn't seem right to him, or just for kicks, he would have us drop and give him pushups or make us do seven-point burpees in full backpacks. There were a few platoons, each with a different assigned drill instructor. Ours seemed to be the meanest of the bunch. We thought he must have been a young, Vietnam-hardened veteran. The yelling didn't bother me, since it wasn't much more than I'd heard from my football coaches. However, here there was no place to go to get away from it until you closed your eyes to sleep at night. By the end of bootcamp, I was able to do 100 push-ups and 100 sit-ups.

On one of the first few days of training, we were marched to a building where we were to take a battery of tests to see what job we were suited for in the Army. During the process, we heard an enlistment speech. A sergeant said we could pick our own job if we enlisted on the spot. I was thinking, "As long as I'm going to do this, I might as well pick something exciting." I mentioned to the guy in line behind me that "door gunner on a helicopter sounds like fun." Looking back, that seems like a very naive thing to say, even for a 20-year-old.

His reply was, "Those guys have the highest mortality rate of any job." So at that point, I thought it best if I took my chances and let my test scores determine what job I would have.

I kept thinking of the words my brother-in-law told me when, on a forced march carrying heavy packs and our M16 rifles, one of the recruits dropped on the march and died on the spot. We were allowed to attend his funeral held on the fort, but I realized my brother-in-law was wrong. Not only *could* they kill us, but they did kill one of us.

Somewhere in the middle of training, I developed a rash across my chest. I reported to the watch commander that I had the rash and was burning up with fever. When I lifted my T-shirt to show him, he leaped from his chair and backed across the room. He quickly arranged to have someone take me to the hospital. Turned out, I had the three-day measles. It gave me a short break from training. Even though I was feeling poorly, the hospital staff had me get out of bed, change the sheets and tuck the corners every day like my barracks bunk. I then had to stand at attention, next to my bed, while they inspected it, before I could get back in it.

Back with my platoon, we would periodically get inspections of our quarters, bunks and foot lockers. We were instructed to stand at attention next to our footlockers. Leonard, Roger, Dave and I stood as directed, but we were in the four-man room, not the larger barracks. We could hear the drill instructor going off on the recruits in the dorm, so I closed the door to our room so gently that it didn't make a noise.

We still stood at attention, as instructed, while the DI was going off on the other recruits. When the DI was done with the guys in the dorm, he stomped downstairs. He completely missed us. Either he forgot about us or didn't know we were even there. We followed this routine for every inspection, and never once did he come into our little room. We were lucky guys.

One of the recruits, a draftee like me, did not want to be in the Army, so he drank Brasso metal polish straight out of the can. He was rushed to the hospital but was back with us the next day. This same guy later pocketed an M-16 round from one of our trips to the rifle range. When we were back at the barracks, cleaning our weapons, he loaded the round in his M-16. Seeing this, the guys around him jumped him before he could do whatever it was he was planning. The DI came in and took this fellow away, and we never saw him again.

Graduation day was nearing, and word had gotten out that our mean SOB of a drill instructor was not a Vietnam veteran. In fact, he wasn't even a sergeant. He was a corporal who had temporary sergeant stripes. He hadn't been in the Army very long at all. As luck would have it, I had KP duty again when the guys in the barracks planned a party for the DI. The DI came into the large dorm, a few guys threw a blanket over him, and they all proceeded to pound on him. The DI was not seen during the last few days of bootcamp, and someone else took his place. Nothing was ever said to us about the incident. He was just gone. I guess this was the bootcamp equivalent of a fragging.

Chapter 19

Soldier Takes a Wife

Graduation day was finally arrived, I had turned 21 in boot camp, and I was ready for some time off. The recruits were gathered in the large dorm as one of the DI's was going to read our names and tell us what our Military Occupational Specialty (MOS) was. He read a name off and then the MOS. Almost everyone was getting 11B, infantryman. I knew that meant they were going to Vietnam. When he got to my name he read, "Cunningham, 92Y supply clerk." I couldn't believe my ears. I was one lucky guy. Leonard and Roger also got 92Y, and we ended up going to Supply Clerk School right there at Fort Ord. Albuquerque Dave got infantry, and we never saw him again.

It was around Christmas, and I had a couple of weeks off after boot camp before going to my advanced training in supply. I had told Debbie that I still didn't know where I would end up being stationed, but if it was Vietnam, we would wait to get married. If it were anywhere else, we would get married, so that she could join me at my duty station.

My supply class was about two months long and all classroom work, a welcome change from bootcamp. Supply school ended, and everyone had been cut orders to their duty stations. That is, except for Leonard, Roger and I. No orders were cut, so we were in limbo. We were assigned to a "holding" company at Fort Ord. We slept in smaller barracks, ate in the mess hall, then assembled each morning, where a sergeant would assign us busy-work.

We painted rocks and swept the grounds, mostly; sometimes we would be trucked to a building and told to move furniture and files around. The sergeant would then dismiss us with orders to "stay low," since sometimes it was still the middle of the day. We went to the bowling alley or movie house sometimes, but mostly stayed in our barracks. After weeks of this routine, Leonard, Roger and I approached the unit commander. The commander was a lieutenant, but he had captain's bars sitting on his desk near his nameplate. I presumed that he was anticipating a promotion soon. I asked permission to talk.
"Granted."

"Sir, the three privates have been waiting three weeks for duty station orders. Is there any way we can speed it up, sir?" In hindsight, we should have kept quiet, as it was easy duty, and no one hassled us. Within a couple of days, orders were cut. All three of us were going to Fort Sill, Oklahoma, to be supply clerks. We all had been promoted to private first class in the process.

Time to call Debbie and set the date. March 23 was to be our wedding date, and it was only a couple weeks away. Because of the speed of the wedding, I'm sure everyone thought she was pregnant. We had just enough time for the wedding and a short honeymoon before I had to be in Oklahoma.

It was great to be in Debbie's warm embrace again, I was one lucky young man. The ceremony was in the same Methodist church where we met just a little more than four years earlier. Our time together was short before I had to fly off to Oklahoma.

I had arranged to met Leonard at the airport, and off to Oklahoma City we went. The flight was followed by a 100-mile bus ride to Lawton. The bus apparently was also on a newspaper route, because we stopped in every town along I-44 to drop off papers.

Leonard and I took a cab from the bus station to the front gate and walked on to our respective duty stations.

I reported to the first sergeant and handed him my orders.
"What the hell, I don't need another Supply Clerk. I have too many now. Look, Private Cunningham, you are now a Finance Clerk (MOS 36B), how does that suit you."

"Sir, that fits the private just fine, sir."
The sergeant told me where the finance building was and that I was to report first thing in the morning. I told him that I was now married and would be looking for housing off the fort.

"Private Cunningham, if the Army had wanted you to have a wife, they would have issued you one" was his reply. I was shown where to bunk and dismissed to the mess hall.

I was more than a little shocked to find the mess hall was serving beer on-tap with the evening meals. This was to be the new Army. They were transitioning to an all-volunteer Army, and they were making changes to attract people to join.

Morning came, and I reported to finance, a single-story wooden building probably dating back to before WWII. This department was being run by a civilian, so now I wasn't even directly working for a military person. Yet again, I was one lucky soldier. I was next sent to a two-week long crash-course on a new computerized finance system that they were just starting.

Chapter 20

A Somewhat Normal Life

On the first weekend in Oklahoma, I walked to town and bought a bike to get around on. I also rented an apartment just a few blocks from the front gate to Fort Sill. I called Debbie and asked her to make arrangements to join me as soon as possible. She flew in a few days later and had her car shipped to us later. I was able to get neighbors to drive me to the airport to greet her, since I didn't have a car yet.

Not having much money, I had not bought sheets for the bed. I apologized and told her I had been sleeping in my government-issued sleeping bag. When Debbie opened her suit case, the first thing she pulled out were sheets for the bed. What a lucky guy, boy, did I marry the right girl! Such a lucky guy!

Leonard was married as well and had two kids, who all joined him in Lawton as well. We hung together sometimes, when we were off duty. That is, until the time I caught him doing angel dust. Angel dust was a street name for PCP back in those days. I didn't need the kind of trouble that came with associating with someone on drugs, particularly while I was in the military.

Army life was now fun. Debbie was with me, and we had developed other friends, Mike and Betty, among others. Mike also worked in finance and was known as "Big Mike," whereas I was "Little Mike," for reasons that were obvious to all. Betty had taken a job as a teacher in Lawton. In the meantime, Debbie got a job as a checker at the local TG&Y. We had normal work weeks, while weekends were spent with friends bowling, at the drive-in or at the speedway watching dirt cars race. Life was good.

I made Specialist 4 after a couple of months. Then one day, while at the office, I received a call from headquarters. I had not had any contact with them since my first week in Oklahoma. Turns out Oklahoma's weather is similar to that of Vietnam, so it became a spot were soldiers would go to on the way to or from Vietnam. The company clerk said, "You came down on orders."

My heart sank. Vietnam! The clerk said, "You came down on orders for Germany." I was elated at the prospect. He continued, "They were for Supply Clerk."

"Hey, that's OK with me!"

"I told them you were a finance clerk now, so they rescinded the orders."

Damn, I sure would have loved to live in Germany with Debbie for a year, but Oklahoma with Debbie was better than 'Nam without her.

Time went by fast in Oklahoma, and I had an office job that did not seem all that military, except I had to wear a uniform to work. After being in Oklahoma for eight months, a rumor went around that the Army was going all professional and would be giving "early outs" to all draftees. Sure enough, I was told that I would be released in April. It was a full six months early.

My discharge interview came up, and I was told that they would make me a sergeant if I re-enlisted. I told them, "I would have to be an officer to re-enlist."

The answer came, "We can arrange that, too."

"Sir, thank you, but no thanks. I had plans before being called to serve, sir." In reality, I had very little idea what I was going to do with my life at that point. My processing out was interrupted when I was told my hair was too long. One last chance to screw with me, but if getting a haircut was all that stood between Debbie and I going home, a haircut it was.

My duty done, and satisfied that I had made Oklahoma safe from the ravages of Communism, Debbie and I drove home in our VW camper van we bought while in Oklahoma. During the trip home we stoped for fuel in Texas. The gas station attendant would not let us buy gasoline. He stated he didn't serve hippies. How ironic, I had just completed my service obligation, and he thought I was a hippie because I drove a van. That is how divided the country was at the time.

Chapter 21

You Can't Go Home Again

Once we got back to California, I found that my mom and dad had divorced. The beautiful home in Rolling Hills Estates was gone, my parents broke. My mother had fled to the desert in Hesperia, California, with my sister, Kerry. My dad was in an apartment in Harbor City, Ken was at college in San Bernardino, and Dave was in an apartment in Lomita. Nothing would ever be the same.

Apparently, after a few moon landings, government contracts for aerospace companies dried up. This led to widespread layoffs in the industry. The lack of income put stress on my parents that the marriage could not endure. This would later turn out to be another factor in my decision to become a firefighter. It would prove to be a stable job with a retirement guaranteed.

I inquired about my old job as a draftsman/illustrator. They took me back, and I immediately enrolled at Long Beach State part-time. Debbie went back to her job as a grocery checker. I had finally decided on a direction: I was aiming on being a teacher. The schedule of a full-time job and part-time schooling was taking its toll, however. I was having stomach pain that the doctor described as "pre-ulcerous." Something had to change.

My brother Dave happened to mention that he had thought about being a fireman at one point and gave me a textbook on the subject, since he had ultimately decided against the profession.

"Of course, a fireman, that's what I really wanted to be since I was a 7-year-old Cub Scout, taking a tour of a fire station." I just had forgotten about it, is all. I enrolled in fire science classes at Harbor Junior College and started taking firefighter entrance examinations. I saw that my dad didn't fare well after being released, following years in the aerospace industry, without a pension. Being a firefighter wouldn't make me rich, but it seemed exciting, offered job security and a retirement.

Being a little naive, I figured it would be easy, I would just walk into a station, fill out an application and become a firefighter. At the first test I took, I saw over 2,000 people waiting to take the exam. Apparently, the television show *Emergency* was a big reason why the job had become so popular.

The tests started with a written exam. If you passed that, you would go on to a physical agility test, and if you passed that, an oral interview. Candidates who passed all three phases were put on an eligibility list, based on their scores. All this for just a very few job openings.

I took 13 tests in a span of 13 months before I scored high enough to get a second interview.

I took a written exam for one city on a Saturday morning. The candidates were told to come back at noon to see who was going on to the physical agility that same afternoon. I felt confident because I had seen that written test before. My name was on the list, so I was able to move on to the physical portion. Those of us who passed the physical agility that afternoon were handed appointment slips for the oral interview starting on Monday morning.

My interview was scheduled for Tuesday. When the interview was done I felt good, especially since they asked, "When can you start?"

"How about tomorrow?" was my answer. Turns out, they asked everyone that question because the academy was starting on Monday. Two days later, I got a call to be interviewed by the assistant chief, and I needed to be in his office as soon as I could. I was there in 30 minutes, coming from work in a nearby city.

After the short interview, where I didn't even get a chance to sit down, I was asked to be ready because the academy was starting on Monday. That happened to be my birthday ... what a present! I turned 21 in bootcamp, and I was going to turn 25 in the Fire Academy. They hired eight people that day, and I had scored high enough to place third on a test that had started with almost 2,000 people. One lucky young man.

I excitedly called Debbie at work and told her I had been hired by the fire department. She was happy too, throughout the rest of her shift. A customer coming through her line at the grocery store commented that Debbie looked happy.

"I am, my husband just got hired by the fire department."

"Oh, fantastic! What department?"

Debbie told her the department's name.

"My husband works for that department, too. Congratulations, what a coincidence!"

With eight of us hired, or at least tentatively hired, we were scheduled for pre-hire physicals the next morning. I was hoping all the while that they would not find out that I had taken seizure medicine as a child. They didn't, and now we had just Friday afternoon and Saturday to buy our uniforms before our Monday morning academy.

I figured the academy was going to be less challenging than bootcamp. Less yelling and more classroom, plus I would get to go home to Debbie every night. Problem was, I was not in as good a shape after working in an office the past four years. I was also fighting off a cold.

During the first afternoon workout, we were run around the training site, then up a ladder, into a window of the training tower, down the stairs and around the site again. On about the third lap, after stepping into the tower I got light-headed and then passed out into the arms of a fellow trainee.

My battalion chief was called to come get me. I was devastated, my first day was going to be my last day. It appeared my lucky streak was about to end. Happy birthday, Mike!

I was taken to the hospital where an ER doctor examined me and said that it was a combination of excitement of my first day and the flu that got the best of me. It was near the end of the day, and the chief told me to go home, but to report back to the academy in the morning. I reported back the next morning, to the surprise of the other candidates, and nervously sailed through the rest of the time, academically and physically.

Chapter 22

A Dream Job and Two Sons

On to our duty stations. Eighteen years later, the dreams of a 7-year-old had come to fruition. My assignment was going to be Station 2 on the A shift. We were expected to learn the city streets by filling out a blank map, memorize equipment use and location, and emergency medical procedures. No one was allowed to watch television on duty that first year. If we had any spare time, it was spent cleaning equipment and studying. I had re-enrolled in college prior to completing probation, taking fire science courses, so some of my nighttime study involved my homework.

My very first call was a full cardiac arrest. A senior citizen had been walking down the street and suddenly passed out, never to regain consciousness. My first fire would come a couple of shifts later. It was a garage fire in the middle of the day, on a Saturday, and I was the lone nozzle man. The fire was started when the owner spilled gas while filling his lawn mower. The fumes then were ignited by the water heater.

Nobody knows what it is really like to be a firefighter, other than another firefighter. Being a firefighter, it turns out, is not so much what you do; it is more like who you are or who you become. Neighbors know you're a firefighter and come to you on your days off with little home problems, injuries or other minor emergencies.

The neighborhood kids know you're a firefighter and tend to hang out at your home with your kids. I suppose knowing that an adult is sometimes home during week days plays a factor.

Many people still think firefighters hang out at the station and play checkers all day. In talking with the guys who were "old timers" when I hired on, that may have been partially true back before the early 1970's. Firefighting has changed over the years. Yes, they still put water on the fire (or put the wet stuff on the red stuff, as one captain was fond of saying), but building construction has changed. More and more hazardous materials are being manufactured and placed on the streets. Firefighters also face the hazards of chemicals in homes due to the proliferation of meth labs.

Firefighting was once just that, fighting fires. Now it has evolved into handling complex medical emergencies with the implementation of the paramedic program. Since that time, fire departments have had to develop experts in hazardous materials, swift water rescue, urban search and rescue, fire investigation, public education, fire prevention and helicopter operations, among others.

Most paid firefighters work 24 hours on and 24 hours off, with a total of 10 shifts worked a month. That may not sound like a lot of days worked, but it's a 56-hour work week, and most firefighters work overtime and/or second jobs.

Firefighters have to work on Christmas, holidays, birthdays and anniversaries. On their off days, they are subject to being ordered back to work. This is an overtime that can't be refused. It doesn't matter whether it happens on your 25th wedding anniversary or not. Somebody has to fill that vacant spot or come in to supplement manpower for a fire, riot, flood or other emergency, and if it's your turn, it's your turn.

Fires don't occur every day within your district. If they did, the community would have burned down in just a few months. Economically speaking, it would be cheaper, in a bedroom community, not to have a fire department. You could let the occasional dwelling burn down completely, and have the city reimburse the owners for their loss rather than pay for equipment and manpower for every day of the year.

Firefighters, however, aren't on duty just for those big fires. They are on duty for the more humane reasons, such as preserving life, saving personal items, and medical emergencies. Medical emergencies account for over 90 percent of the calls they go on now.

Firefighters are a strange breed because, while they don't wish a fire on anyone, they do want to be on duty when a big one occurs. That, after all, is what they trained for. I guess, in a way, they are adrenalin junkies.

If a fire happens late at night, the dirty hose is just left rolled up behind the fire station. The on-coming shift would get a little jealous, knowing they would have to clean the hose but had no hand in fighting the fire.

I was hired as a fireman but had to turn that badge in for one that read "firefighter," because that was more politicly correct, once women showed interest in the profession.

When I started as a fireman, we rode to fires on the tailboard at the rear of the engine. This meant that we could not finish suiting up for a fire until we arrived on scene. Putting on an air pack while in front of a burning structure gets a firefighter's adrenalin pumping in direct proportion to the size of the fire and task that lies before them.

Fire engines have now evolved to the point where everyone is in an enclosed cab, with air packs that can be readily available prior to arriving on scene.

My favorite jobs were on the hose line, the nozzle person, or the captain charged with leading the crew on fire attack. This meant that we were going to be the first people in the building with a hose line. Interior firefighting resembles nothing like what you've seen in movies like *Backdraft, Ladder 49* or any of the television series. Once inside the structure, the smoke is so thick you can't see two feet in front of your face mask.

In many instances, they're on their bellies dragging the hose behind them. They do this to avoid the heat and heaviest smoke.

Once inside the building, firefighters don't indiscriminately spray water at everything they see. They have to make their way through the building until they see the glow of the fire. When the water is finally applied, the fire can go out in quick fashion if the flames are contained to one room.

With interior fires comes the danger of being steam-burned around the neck, ears and wrists. This happens when water they are applying turns the entire room into a super-heated steam bath. Protective clothing has come a long way over the years as well, and firefighters now have fire-resistant clothing, hoods to protect their ears, and better gloves. This poses another problem however, because with all the protective clothing, firefighters don't know how hot it is getting until their helmets start to melt around their faces.

The job I liked least was the task of roof ventilation. This chore is given to the truck companies. That is the longer vehicles with a ladders on them. Engines have a water tank, a pump and the hose. Trucks typically have no hose or a water tank. What they do have, is equipment and manpower. They are like a rolling tool box. The truck company is charged with ventilating the structure to rid it of the smoke and heat so that the engine company (firefighters with the hose) can see and better find the fire.

Ventilation often requires firefighters to go to the roof of a structure and cut a large hole in it. I never liked this job, because you can't see the fire. However, the job requires that you cut a hole over or as near to the fire as you can. Firefighters are actually right over the most dangerous portion of the building at that moment. My guess is that we have lost more firefighters to roof operations than we have to interior firefighting. I once heard a chief say that he would "rather have his sister be a hooker than to marry a B-shift trucker." I'm not sure what he had against the B shift, but I understand the truck part.

The hardest part of the job has to be telling someone that a loved one has died. This can be conveyed to the deceased's loved ones in a number of ways, but a policy came out near the end of my career that required you to use the word "dead." We never received a class or direction other than use of the word "dead." It seemed so much colder the first time I had to tell an 11-year-old that her mother was "dead." I never followed that policy after that.

Despite the injuries, the long hours and missed Christmases, I would not have traded those 30 years for another job. I was one lucky firefighter.

My wife and I had been waiting for me to land a job with a fire department before having children. With the first requirement fulfilled, we were blessed to have James (Jimi) come into our lives. We were then a family, and family is what I have come to cherish most in life.

Soon I had my Associate of Arts degree in fire science. I then learned that Cal State Los Angeles had a public administration program designed for firefighters, so I enrolled in that. After a couple of semesters, I was chosen to attend paramedic school, so I had to drop my classes once again.

Paramedic school was to be held at Harbor General Hospital, the same location where the TV show *Emergency* was filmed. The classes were affiliated with UCLA medical school.

Paramedic school consisted of two months of intense classroom training, with daily tests, two months of hospital and classroom work, more tests, and two months field work with active paramedics. My mom had moved to Carson, California, by that time, and I was able to stay with her those first two months. This cut down travel time, so that I could study at night rather than fight traffic to and from Diamond Bar, where we had purchased our first home. I would go home on Fridays and spend weekends with my wife and son. My graduating class was during just the fourth or fifth year of the paramedic program. My first call as a certified paramedic, like my first call as a firefighter, was a full cardiac arrest.

With paramedic school behind me, a second son, Jared, was born. I surely was one lucky and blessed man.

Intent on continuing my education, I re-enrolled at Cal State Los Angeles before I even finished my paramedic field training.

Within a few more semesters, I had my B.S. in public administration. I thought I was done with school when another firefighter asked me to teach fire science at El Camino College right after I graduated Cal State. With all the interruptions it had taken me twelve years to get through college, now I was teaching it.

Chapter 23

The Station

Firefighters see some pretty horrific stuff during the course of their careers. To fight off stress or trauma, they all seem to develop a good sense of humor. This humor may seem macabre to the casual observer.

Firefighters, for the most part, will remain professional while on the scene of a dismemberment, decapitation or other grizzly sight, only to return to the station and joke about it. It beats crying all the time. Besides, the next call may be only a fews minutes away, and they'll just have to put on their game face once again.

Firefighters pull pranks on each other from time to time, but this practice seems to have slowed down somewhat in recent years, due to fears of discrimination or harassment charges. It used to be that if you were not given a nickname or had pranks pulled on you, you probably were not liked.

I was known as Killer, so named after an arm wrestling victory in the academy. It was a name I did not particularly care for. As one might imagine, when I became a paramedic, patients were alarmed whenever they heard me called by my nickname. I was later known as Shadow when I became an Arson Investigator, Shadow being Robert DeNiro's part in the movie *Backdraft*. One firefighter named Dick was asked what nickname he would like to go by. After a few moments he said, *"Dick will do."* From that point on, he was known as Dick-el-do.

One of my pranks on a fellow firefighter was to put a spring-loaded fake snake in a glass container of pancake mix. We waited days until the unsuspecting target finally opened the container. The snake sprang out as planned and completely covered his fresh uniform in pancake mix. We laughed hysterically at the sight of him as he grabbed a fork and repeatedly stabbed the snake in some sort of revenge.

The cruelest — and perhaps funniest — prank in the station took weeks in planning. One firefighter who was between marriages and had been dating a lot of women. AIDS was new, and little was known about the virus it at the time. This fellow was a worrier and asked the paramedics from time to time how one would know if he had AIDS.

One day, the paramedics came into the station with test tubes. Each had a label with the names of the individual firefighters on them. The medics said it was a new test for AIDS, and that we were all to take the test. The firefighters had to take a Q-tip and swab their gums, then place the swab in the test tubes. In the bottom of the tubes was a yellow substance that would turn red if you had AIDS.

All of the tubes had Dijon mustard in them, with the exception of one. That one had a substance that was the same color, but it was used to test oil to see if it contained water. The substance turned red when exposed to water.

So each firefighter took his turn swabbing his gums and placing the Q-tip in the tubes. When it was our victim's turn, the substance turned red immediately. He tossed the tube across the room, smashing it against the wall and shouted, "I knew it, I knew it, I have AIDS! And I only did it once!"

We were all stunned, and to this day, I am not sure what he meant by "only did it once." Whatever he did once, and with whom, was none of my business. He was allowed to call his partner(s) to let them know. Hours passed before someone was brave enough to let him in on the prank.

Despite pranks that sometimes bordered on being cruel, station life was fun. The crew had a routine that would be interrupted only by fires, medical calls and other emergencies.

The on-coming shift would arrive a little early to place their personal stuff on the engine, truck, squad or whatever rig they were assigned to for the shift, then check out the equipment. They would then make their way to the kitchen to grab a cup of coffee and hear from the off-going shift what was new and what had happened the shift before.

Next was line-up, an informal meeting around the table to brief the crew for what was planned for the day. These plans could include station tours, fire prevention inspections, drills or other activity. All plans, of course, were subject to change due to emergency calls. The number of calls varied and could be more than 20 calls in a single 24-hour shift for a paramedic unit.

Line-up is followed by a workout session, a shower, then dressed for the day. A cook is assigned on a rotating basis, and the vehicle they are assigned to would make the store run. Lunch is followed by a card game or two to determine who does the dishes. This process is repeated for the dinner meal.

I picked up a bad habit that follows me today. I eat much too fast. I eat fast because most every meal would be interrupted by a call. If you're gone more than just a few minutes, the meal is cold when you get back and not worth reheating in a microwave.

When a firefighter is new, every call is new and exciting, but the more experienced firefighters see little new, and they know the best part of the job is in the station and the people you work with.
Most firefighters will never forget their first call, first fire, and their last call. But for many of them, including me, everything else seems like a blur, with the exception of the anecdotes in this book.

Long before it became time to retire, I knew I would miss the guys (I never had the chance to work with a female firefighter) much more than the adrenalin of the calls.

Chapter 24

Ghosts

Firefighters all have ghosts that they must cope with from time to time. We try hard to leave work at work and home at home, so that we don't burden our families with what we see and have to deal with on a daily basis. We hate to see a child hurt in any way. We can try to separate it from home, but somehow we think of our own kids who may be the same age as a patient.

One such call I was on had a 4-year-old girl who ran out into the parking lot of the apartment she lived in. She just wanted to say goodbye to her uncle, who was already in his car. He tragically backed over her head.

I knew she was gone when I arrived, but you keep thinking a miracle could happen, and you want the family to know that you did everything humanly possible to save that precious little life. I thought that might give them some comfort, however little it may be. The child was transported to the closest hospital, with CPR in progress, where she was pronounced dead on arrival. This is one such ghost I carry with me.

Two other ghosts gave me nightmares for years, and both happened on the same shift. The first was a jumper. This mid-30's male apparently wanted to end it all by jumping into a concrete canal 60 feet below.

The jump was later described by a witness in a nearby restaurant. The witness stated that the jumper just fell head first into the canal and did not even appear to put his arms out or take any other defensive action.

I was on the rescue that day, so my partner and I had to rappel into the canal to check treat the patient. The drug box and EKG monitor were lowered down to us. The patient's head was opened, and brain-matter was showing. This alone would allow us to determine "no signs of life."

To double check, I hooked up the EKG monitor to the patient. At this point, the incident commander yelled down, "Is he dead?" The monitor showed a rhythm that indicated that he wasn't dead. My partner looked at me. We looked at the monitor, then we looked at each other again. My partner shouted up, "He's dead!"

With that, the EKG monitor went straight line. It was as if the patient's soul was standing over us, waiting for us to confirm that he had died.

Later, in the same shift, a horrific accident occurred where a vehicle burst into flames after impact. The vehicle was extinguished by the engine company, which also put out a smaller fire a few yards away from the vehicle.

The smaller fire had been the vehicle's occupant. After the impact, he must have been alive and either ran from or was thrown from the vehicle while on fire and died just a few yards from the accident site. He had total-body third degree burns, and I pronounced him dead at the scene.

I've never been diagnosed with post traumatic stress, but I wouldn't be surprised, with all the ghosts and everything else that firefighters have to see and do, if it hasn't left me with a touch of it.

Chapter 25

Drugs and the Naked Lady

My favorite calls, as a medic, were the diabetic and drug overdose calls. This is because the drugs paramedics carry can quickly counteract what was happening to the patient and wake them up or bring them back to life before your eyes. Narcan is given for drug overdoses, and D50 (sugar water) for diabetics.

I always got a big kick out of finding a heroin OD down, breathing just two to four times a minute, and a new officer or firefighter on scene with me. Basically, the patient is circling the drain and would die shortly if it weren't for our intervention. As soon as the IV is established, Narcan is pushed, and the near-death OD is up and talking. These patients were never grateful, but often seemed ticked off that we ruined a good high.

The look on the face of a new officer or firefighter is priceless when the patient bolts upright, like something from a zombie film. I quickly learned that you restrain the patient prior to giving the Narcan, or they might run away.

I once dropped off a drug OD patient at the hospital after having given Narcan. As we were restocking the rescue rig, the patient bolted from the hospital bed, ran out through doors of the hospital, past the rescue rig and out into the night. This would have been funnier except we knew the Narcan would wear off, the patient would drop, and we would once again be called out.

Once upon a time, PCP was a drug of choice, and we could tell when a new batch hit the street, because our call load of drug ODs would increase. One of my first PCP overdose patients, according to his roommate, came home in the middle of the night but did not make it to bed. When the roommate awoke, he found the patient still standing naked in the middle of the room, having been frozen in that place since the night prior.

With PCP patients, you must move very slowly, so as not to startle them. In today's world, this patient would be transported via ambulance to the nearest hospital, but back then, it was permissible to transport them via police vehicle. This is safer for the medics, because these people are capable of superhuman strength. I wanted them in cuffs and inside a caged vehicle.

The fire crew and several police officers picked up the patient who was as rigid as a statue and laid him lengthwise in the back of the patrol car, with the patient moving not so much as one muscle.
Over the years, I had one repeat customer who used PCP as her drug of choice. I was aware of her since she was about 16 years old and had been gang-raped while she was asleep in a sleeping bag outside her trailer home. It seemed that after this event, she started using PCP.

Every firefighter and medic in town knew this young lady. How could they not? Several times a month, we would find her lying in the street butt-naked, dusted on PCP.

One of the firefighters struggled with our concept of "leave home at home and work at work." He tried to counsel the young woman and wanted to get her off the street and out of her environment. After long talks with his wife and family, he brought her home to his mountain cabin. While things appeared to work for a day or two, she relapsed and ran from the mountain cabin barefoot through three feet of snow. She missed her old life, apparently, and I would respond to calls on her a few more times, as she lay naked in the street, dusted on PCP.

The last time I saw her, she looked like a straight but a somewhat burned-out woman in her mid 30's. She had married a man about 45 years her senior. They were living in a very old single-wide mobile home, and it looked as if they may have been hoarders. Our patient that day was her husband, who was ill. She pulled a firefighter aside and told him, "Someday, all this will be mine." Wherever you are, I wish you well, Ms. K.

Chapter 26

Bambi and Champagne

Every city of any considerable size has areas that are worked by ladies of the night. Like these ladies, firefighters are frequently on the street when most good people are fast asleep. Firefighters know all too well which are the better and which are the worse areas of the city. Two local characters went by the names Bambi and Champagne.

These working ladies gave me no particular trouble. Champagne would hike her dress over her head when the rescue drove by late at night, just for our entertainment, apparently.

Bambi, on the other hand, was the one trouble seemed to follow. She had only one eye. I never learned how she had lost the eye. At one point, Bambi got married to someone who gave her grief by being in trouble with the law. He eventually was shot and killed in the middle of a busy street. I heard later that she, too, was shot and killed for unknown reasons.

The city council members had their eyes opened to the problem of prostitution by an officer who, while in a patrol car, filmed an interview with one of these ladies. The prostitute pulled off her top and flashed the camera just for the fun of it. When the council saw this film, the police started to run sting operations in an effort to run off the johns (customers).

Female police officers, late at night, would dress like the "ladies" and walk the street, fishing for johns to bust. Coming from a tight-knit department, I knew every police officer on the job at one point. Late one night, while driving back to the station from one of my calls, I saw an officer walking the street. I honked the horn, flipped on my lights and waved at her.

I thought nothing else of the event until the next shift, when the fire chief called me into his office and said that a citizen had complained that I was flirting with prostitutes.

Chapter 27

Shootout at the Nudie Bar

The area where I worked wasn't the nicest of areas, and shootings were not all that unusual. I once responded to a sprained ankle at a shopping center, just around the corner from the station. When the rescue pulled up in front of the store, we heard gun shots. My partner floored the gas pedal, laying rubber as we speed away. Looking in the side mirror, I could see, not 20 feet from the back of our rescue, two young men had been gunned down at close range.

Police, in big numbers, quickly arrived and cleared the scene for us to return. The two men had minor injuries to their legs. Just another day in paradise! Oh, the ankle injury turned out to be minor as well.

Late one night, I was dispatched to another shooting. I thought nothing of it, again since we saw a lot of shootings. When I arrived, I had to call in a lot more units for what had been a simple one-victim shooting turned out to be a big shootout at a nudie bar.

I was dealing with victims down in the street, in the doorway and inside the bar. My partner and I preformed triage. When you have multiple patients and only a few caregivers, the first arriving medics are taken out of the care-giving loop. They just have to quickly access damage and determine what additional resources are needed. We declared two dead at the scene and four others who needed help; two were in critical shape.

I later found a rookie trying to resuscitate one of the victims that I had declared dead and covered with a sheet. I told him, "You can't save them all, go help the living." That rookie later went on to be a great medic and captain.

The patients were treated and sent to various hospitals, where one more died. I returned to the scene to talk with police officers who were still sorting out what had happened.

Apparently, a bar customer had been eighty-sixed (kicked out) from the bar. He returned some time later with a gun and began shooting into the bar. Many of the patrons were carrying weapons of their own (it was a rough neighborhood) and began shooting back. Two armed guards were shooting, customers were shooting, and the bad guy was shooting.

The bad guy was dead in the street, along with a customer. Another customer died in the hospital, while two guards and an additional customer received non-fatal wounds. Many of the shooters just disappeared into the night.

Chapter 28

Brush Fires

As a city firefighter, I didn't get in on a lot of brush fires. However, I did get sent from my Southern California station to Red Bluff, some 60 miles from the Oregon border, along with a strike team of several other fire engines from surrounding cities.

We traveled all night, not sure of where we would be working, since fires were burning in Yosemite and Red Bluff, along with several other areas within the state. Resources were short and spread thin because big fires were burning in other states as well that year.

We arrived in Sacramento and were immediately redirected to the Red Bluff fire. A couple of more hours of traveling, and we were at the command post. We were immediately dispatched to a two-lane road with the directive to keep the fire from jumping the road. The fire raged up a hill toward us, burning tree tops at first, as it skipped across a forested area. Then entire group of trees seemed to explode into flame.

The midday sky grew dark, and our crew couldn't see our hands in front of our faces. We sprayed water into the darkness, then into the direction of the engines and onto each other to spare ourselves from the heat.

The sky suddenly cleared, and the fire had moved far down

the other side of the road we were on. It had jumped us as if we weren't even there. We were disappointed that we had failed in our task, but extremely happy that we came out of it unscathed.

We were later reassigned to a cul-de-sac of homes that were surrounded by tall pines. Our mission was to protect the homes from the advancing fire. The first thing I noted when we arrived was that there was no safety zone; we had only one way in and that same one way out. I mentioned to my captain that we were in an indefensible location, and we were in danger if we stayed.

The captain listened and took my concerns to the strike-team leader, a chief. Moments later, we were back on the engines and headed out of harm's way.

The strike team later traveled back across this same area of cul-de-sac homes and found the entire area had been devastated by the fire; we would not have gotten out alive had we stayed.

Years later, I suddenly realized that I could no longer do the job I was hired to do while at a different wild-land fire. My back hurt too much, and my leg would go numb to the point that I couldn't get up and down the hills. I thought I was able to hide my difficulties in getting around, even though I would sometimes limp to the squad or engine I was assigned to. When the station captain next had to go to a brush fire, he took a younger man, even though it was my turn to go. Soon after this, I learned from doctors and therapists who read my MRI that my back was so bad that I couldn't return to the job I loved.

Chapter 29

Fire Investigations

The department I worked for had no formal system for conducting fire investigations beyond the engine company level, prior to the "Church Fires." In the early 1980's, the entire southern California area was inundated with church fires, all occurring late at night and usually around the pulpit area. Most fires were set with just available combustibles, but some were accelerated with flammables liquids.

I lost count at around 21 fires. As can be imagined, this became a political and community nightmare. The city I worked for saw several of these fires, and a Buddhist Temple was burned down, then set on fire a second time while it was still in the process of being rebuilt.

Community pressure was mounting, and it was finally decided that our fire department would have trained fire investigators who would work hand-in-hand with police officers. At the same time, a cooperative team of fire investigators was formed, comprising all the area fire departments. This new position was going to require formal and on-the-job training, including ride-a-longs with the police to learn interview techniques and other police procedures. The team eventually qualified with weapons, wrote out arrest warrants, search warrants and filed cases with the DA's office.

During our investigation of the church fires, my police counterpart and I began concentrating on a gang member who lived in our city, but we were never able to catch him at it. We spent many hours on this case, as did investigators in other jurisdictions. In the end, the arsonist turned himself in at the front desk of the police station. He was the father of our original suspect.

This man apparently was deranged, but he eventually found religion. While speaking with clergy, he confessed what he had been doing. Clergy members convinced the suspect to "make things right in this world" and turn himself in, which he did.

The man was tried and sent for psychiatric help, in a location where, I am told, fires soon began breaking out.

In the late 1980's, the Masons started a practice of honoring a firefighter and a police officer with a dinner and a plaque denoting appreciation. In 1992, I was so honored by being named "Firefighter of the Year." It may have been due to my work as a medic, an Investigator, or both. I was very honored.

Chapter 30

Firefighters Down

Most every firefighter encounters that close call, where they come much too close to danger. Perhaps it is luck, skill, intuition or the hand of God that intervenes. Sometimes the intervention doesn't come in time.

My worse fear came on a fire that involved a six-car garage, and I was captain on the first arriving truck. My crew was running out of fire headquarters at the south end of the city. The fire was at the extreme north end of the city, and first arriving engines were reporting a working fire.

The duty battalion chief had given my truck the order to ventilate the building before either I or he had arrived on scene. Sometimes this can mean opening windows, or it can mean cutting a hole in the roof. The fire building was a garage serving an unattached apartment building.

I didn't like the order, because it was always a dangerous assignment. However in this case, it was only a detached garage, no exposures were in danger, and from the involvement, it looked like it was going to be fought from the exterior. Ventilation was not required, in my opinion.

I took my crew to the roof, one with a saw, one with a rubbish hook, and I was up there to access the situation and supervise. The roof was a little weak, but it did not appear to be in danger of burning through anytime soon. No sooner had the third firefighter joined us on the roof when the whole building suddenly failed. The trusses had burned through. The front walls fell outward, causing the engine firefighters to momentarily drop their lines and flee. The roof had fallen into the building, with my crew right over the fire at the time.

With the walls falling outward, the roof fell into the building, forcing us onto our backs. Falling on my breathing apparatus tank, I was sliding down the roof toward the burning fire. Maybe it was God's hand or just plain luck, but the force of the roof falling in seemed to dampen down the fire, and we were lucky that the remaining hot spots were quickly extinguished by the those on the engine company who had picked up their lines again. We were spared from the flames, but not from injury.

All three of us sustained injuries, but thankfully, we were all eventually able to return to work. I, however, am still paying for the event with back pain every minute of every day, despite two back surgeries and two knee surgeries.

Chapter 31

Riots

I was on duty when the criminal trial verdict came in that eventually led to the Rodney King riots. Assigned to the rescue that day, my partner and I were in a fast food store, and an overhead television was about to air a news conference given by Mayor Tom Bradley. We heard him say, "The people have to vent their anger."

I told to my partner, "Oh my God, he's going to incite a riot." To this day, no one laid any blame on who, in my opinion, really started the riot: Mayor Tom Bradley. It wasn't three hours later that riots broke out just a few miles from my station.

Things weren't too bad during my first in-district assignment that night, but when we got off duty the next morning, we were told to stay close to a phone. At the time, I was a board member for a youth baseball league in which one of my sons played. I decided it would be in the kids' best interest if the games were canceled. I didn't think it would be safe in any neighborhood that night.

I was called back to work around 3:30 on the afternoon the riots started. On my way to my station, I was driving north on Vermont Avenue when I observed a lot of people running from a gas station toward a 7-11 store. Two men were tagging the building with graffiti, while others were breaking windows and looting the store.

Being the department's fire investigator, I was allowed to carry a weapon. My 9mm Smith & Wesson was on the seat next to me, and my hand was on it for ready use, should the crowd start to rush my car. The vehicle in front of me, seeing the action in the street, tried to take a left turn against a red light and had a minor accident. I crept through the intersection and continued on my way to the station unmolested.

I spent the next five consecutive days on duty, more than 120 straight hours. Some days I was on an engine, and some days I was on a paramedic unit. I alternated from captain, firefighter, paramedic and back again to whatever the need was. The days seemed to blur together as we went from call to call and tried to catch a little sleep whenever we could.

A citywide curfew was announced, ordering that no one was allowed on the streets after sunset. This seemed to be a joke for many people, but at least we knew that anyone that was out after dark could be considered a bad guy.

We did several days worth of grocery shopping on the first day because we couldn't be sure the market would be standing the next day.

Police officers were stationed in the firehouse with us during the riots. They would respond with us on every call they could, just to protect us. We would try to repay the favor by always having a pot of chili and coffee available for them.

There were times when police officers were not available when we went out on fires. On those occasions, my duty was to stand guard with my 9mm handgun while other members of the company loaded hose back onto the engine.

My station was a few blocks away from a predominately Chinese-owned shopping center. The center was open during daylight hours and sustained no damage at night, even though other businesses on the street were burned, graffitied and looted. It wasn't until the third night, as I was passing the shopping center after a call, that I found out why it was left untouched. Several men were on the roof top, dressed in black ninja garb, wielding rifles and guns. The rioters undoubtedly knew they were there.

During those five days, I went on many fires, with some buildings burning more than once, and even had to drive past some fires to get to others. We had several shootings, although I did not see any fatalities during that time.

Chapter 32

Losing Was Not An Option

I was never good at office politics, though I held the offices of director, treasurer, secretary, vice president and president of the Firefighters Association. I was also a founding member, vice president and president of the Arson Control Team.

When I started my firefighting profession, the city I worked for had a number of casinos that helped keep the city well-funded. In later years, neighboring cities opened casinos, and the players started going to the newer clubs, rather than play in the old ones. Some of the older clubs went out of business, and the city coffers were a little leaner for it.

The city tried to raise money by starting the first municipal insurance company in the state. This venture failed, costing the city a lot of money. Adding to their problems, the city manager, at that time, was tried for embezzling from the city.

To make bad things worse, a city-backed, first-time home buyers program ended with many of the loans in default. The city was in dire straights financially and trying to stay afloat by riding on the backs of its employees.

The city asked the various unions to come up with solutions to the problem. I recommended that the city contract its fire service with the larger Los Angeles County department. A survey later revealed that the city could save $1 million a year over a five-year contract.

The city council initially balked at giving up local control of its fire department. Its answer to the money problem was to threaten lay-offs, in hopes that senior employees would retire, saving junior employees. Even though some firefighters retired, the savings weren't enough, so the city council opted for what we called "rolling blackouts." This meant that manpower would not be constant, and a truck company or paramedic unit could be placed "out of service" on any given day, based on who called in sick or was on vacation.

I convinced the union that contracting with the larger county department was our best option, the city's best option, and in the best interest of the citizens. We took our proposal to the street, gathering signatures to put an initiative on the next ballot.

The city council, still not wanting to give up local control, placed two other initiatives on the ballot; one to keep the fire department local, and another to contract with a larger, neighboring, city.

Their hope was, by having three options, none would get a majority vote, thus it would stay status quo. We campaigned for the county initiative, spending over $50,000 of our own money in ads, fliers and calls to registered voters.

Our county initiative won overwhelmingly over the other two initiatives, but it took over a year-and-a-half for the official handover of employees and equipment to take place.

During exit negotiations, I was asked what I would have done if our initiative had lost. The negotiator was alluding to our possible "political suicide."

"We had not thought about it," I said, "because losing was not an option."

Chapter 33

Barred Windows

It was late enough in the evening, and the whole shift was fast asleep, when an alarm toned out two stations for a fire in a motel. Everyone from my station made their way to the engine and rescue unit. I had been assigned to the rescue as a paramedic that day.

On rescues, I normally headed out of the station before the engine, as it is a little slower than the rescue. On fire calls, I laid back and let the engine lead the way. This was done for two reasons. One, without the engine, paramedics have no way to put water on the fire. Two, I never want to park in the way of the first arriving engine and truck companies, blocking their access to the building.

On this night, the dispatcher gave a second tone: "Responding units, be advised you have a victim trapped on the south side of the building."

Hearing this, I sped out of the firehouse ahead of the engine so I could access the problem and see if I could help in getting the trapped person out of the building.

When these calls come in, firefighters tend to drive a little faster than they would normally. The streets were dry and traffic was clear, so off we sped to the call.

Driving down the street, I could see a large column of smoke from some distance out. As I got closer, I could see the glow of the flames. I was intent on going to the south side of the building, in an attempt to rescue whomever, however I could.

A police officer was standing in the middle of a major four-lane street, waving his arms in air, trying to stop us. I knew I had to go to the south side and wanted very badly to continue to the south side without delay. But I was forced to come to a complete stop because the officer stepped in front of the vehicle I was driving.

After I came to a stop, the officer told me, "Someone is trapped in a room on the south side."

"I know, I know. Step out of the way and let me work."

We finally reached the south side, where horrendous screams could be heard coming from a window that was barred. I could see a person's arms outstretched through the bars. The screaming was frantic. Several police officers were positioned at the window, trying in vain to pull the bars from the stucco wall.

My partner, a hulk of a man who once played linebacker in college football, joined the police officers. If he couldn't pull the bars off with his bare hands, they weren't going to come off that way.

I gave a scene size-up over the radio: "Single-story motel, smoke and flames from the south side, with entrapment. No exposure danger."

I grabbed my breathing apparatus because I knew someone had to go inside that building, and the window area was too crowded already. The screaming continued, increasing the adrenaline flow in all of us.

The engine arrived behind us, as did many more units. I saw an engineer running down the alley with a circular saw. He was intent on cutting the bars just as the screaming subsided. The person behind the bars disappeared into the blackness.

I ran around the building to the front door of the unit that was on fire. A length of fire hose was now lying on the ground near the door while a firefighter was clearing more hose out of the engine hose bed.

I was the first one to put an air pack on, so I grabbed the nozzle just as a firefighter joined me to back me up on the line. We went in very aggressively, trying to make our way toward the back of the unit. The firefighter behind me sustained steam burns to his ears and neck, but he pushed on with me despite his pain.

We found the victim sitting on top of the toilet slumped over, having sustained almost total-body, second-degree burns. The firefighter's muffled words were heard through his facemask: "I think he's dead."

At that moment, the victim took a breath.

"No he's not," I said, and we grabbed the victim, now joined by other firefighters, and we carried him out of the building. Once outside, the victim was cooled with water. I took off my air pack and jacket so that I could intubate the victim (stick a tube down his throat) to better give him oxygen.

My partner rejoined me and started an IV on the victim. I contacted our base hospital to give them patient status and obtain a hospital destination. Off we rushed with CPR in progress on the now-critical patient in the back of the ambulance.

We restocked our medical equipment and returned to the fire scene so that I could conduct the fire investigation. The room was typical of motels with the exterior door leading to the bedroom, living area and a bathroom. What was not typical was that the bathroom windows had bars on them that couldn't be released from the interior.

It led to the needless death of a 35-year-old male, because he chose the wrong motel and appeared to have been drinking and smoking in bed.

The epilogue to this story is that at the next city council meeting, the fire department was accused of taking too long to get to the fire scene, causing the death.

We received no commendations and no apologies. A citizen accused us of taking too long to respond to the fire "because we were pushing to be absorbed into the larger county fire department" at the time. He asserted that we dragged our feet, making our response times seem longer. We were told that we took 20 minutes to get to the fire scene.

In reality, dispatch records showed it took us less than four-and-a-half minutes to get up from a dead sleep, get dressed and arrive at the fire scene. The national average at that time was over five minutes.

The only thing that slowed us down was the excited police officer who was flapping his arms like he was going to take off. I thought we deserved commendations, not accusations.

I was attending the council meeting when the subject of our response time came up and felt compelled to address the citizens and the council, since I was the first arriving firefighter.

I gave the initial fire scene size-up, and after what turned into an emotional and impromptu speech, I heard applause from many in room. I was visibly shaking. A fellow firefighter put his arm around me and led me from the council chambers. I could hear one attendee, as I exited, "That poor firefighter."

I responded to another fire a few days later. I donned my air pack as I had done so many times before, but this time it was different. I was starved for air, I was starting to panic and had trouble calming myself and concentrating on the tasks before me.

I got through it, but I was scared to death that if I couldn't get over this, my career was over. You can't have a firefighter who panics at a fire. You can't be a firefighter and not be able to wear a breathing apparatus.

I kept my problem secret, knowing that my days on the job were numbered, and that number may have just gotten smaller. I made an appointment with my family doctor, who diagnosed me with high blood pressure. The blood pressure was causing shortness of breath, and being short of breath was giving me the anxiety at fires. The doctor prescribed blood pressure medicine, and my symptoms went away. I attribute my blood pressure problems, at least in part, to that city council meeting.

Chapter 34

Helicopters

The last five years on the job were spent with the larger department, Los Angeles County, after we won our political initiative. Coming from a smaller department, I never had the opportunity to work on a fire boat or helicopter. So, at age 51, I had the chance to go to school to learn helicopter operations.

This program is reserved only for paramedics because the helicopters are used for both firefighting and medical calls. The job requires paramedics to be able to rappel down a rope from the helicopter to rescue someone 200 feet or more below. On fires, the medic is dropped off at a remote site and is responsible for filling the helicopter's water and fuel tanks. This portion of the job is muddy, cold and bone weary. Not as glamorous as I had pictured.

During training, the time came for my first rappel from a helicopter, a Firehawk. This is a military helicopter, better known as a Blackhawk, that was outfitted for firefighting and rescue work. As I slid out, I remember thinking to myself, "I'm 51 years old, what in the hell am I doing?" It was so much fun, and the adrenalin rush I had missed was back.

I had gone through training with anticipation of bidding into the position full-time, when or if an opening arose. Additionally, once trained, I could work overtime in the helicopter spot. The bid never opened to me, and I only got to work one eight-hour spot on the helicopter.

However, during that eight-hour spot, I got to work a small brush fire in the mud and cold, and I worked a very bad accident that involved a death, and a very badly injured youth that we transported to a hospital. I also was part of a rescue team in finding a lost and weary hiker in one of the nearby mountains. I was lowered down and then led the hiker over to the helicopter's landing zone. A very busy eight-hour shift, but ultimately, I was sort of glad the full time spot never opened to me.

Chapter 35

September 11, 2001

September 11th will always be a solemn day for firefighters. On that day in 2001, I was at Station 6, in Lomita, scheduled to go off duty at 8 a.m. on the 11th. Lomita was a middle-income city with a mix of residential and commercial sales. The area was much less busy than the city I had been working for.

It had been a normal shift with nothing noteworthy happening, just a few calls during the day and a few more during the night. Around 6 a.m., I was awakened by the sound of one of the other firefighters yelling, "Oh my God! You guys ain't going to believe this shit."

We sat very quietly watching the TV, but we all knew what was happening to our brothers when the first tower collapsed. We lost 343 brothers in the blink of any eye.

County-wide, it was ordered that firefighters who worked on the 10th would be held over on the 11th because we were unsure if planes would start hitting buildings in the Los Angeles area.

We were released four or five hours later, after all aircraft over the country had been grounded, something that had never been done before. The loss of 343 brothers that day will always be locked in our hearts and minds.

I would later transfer to station 119 in Diamond Bar, which I retired out of, but I worked overtime in many different areas across the county, including station 51, where the TV show *Emergency* was filmed. It had been renumbered station 127, because 51 was given to the station at Universal Studios. I even worked a few times at the Palos Verdes fire station. This station was just 75 yards from my first job as a drugstore delivery boy, 38 years earlier.

Chapter 36

Private Investigations

As a certified fire and explosion investigator, I eventually took the state test to become a private investigator, then found a position with a private investigation firm out of Southern California. I worked for that firm for about 11 years, at the same time I was still working for the fire department. My territory stretched from San Luis Obispo to the Mexican border, a 330-mile stretch.

Insurance companies would call the firm to have investigations done on buildings, autos and boats, to find out how a fire started. This was done to determine or fix liability for the loss. The bottom line was who would pay for the loss. This sometimes meant that I would have to testify in court.

After retiring from the fire department and leaving the firm, I teamed up with a long-time friend who also had worked for the previous firm. We formed our own partnership, working the same Southern California areas.

He had a license that would allow him to investigate fires in California. I had a license that allowed me to investigate fires in California, Oregon and Washington. We operated two separate offices after I moved to Washington, so my partner worked out of California, while I worked the Pacific Northwest. This turned out to a lot of fun, and it never felt like work because it was something we enjoyed doing.

At age 60, I required two back surgeries for previous fire department-related injuries, and later two knee surgeries. This proved to be the end of the line for my private career. However, I couldn't help but think that I had been one lucky guy.

Part III

Memorable calls

Sometimes Truth is Stranger Than Fiction

Chapter 37

It Only Hurts When I Laugh

The human animal is very fragile, more so than most other animals, I think. The best thing we have going for us is our intelligence, so it's no wonder that accidents happen when people aren't thinking.

THUMP THUMP

I once responded to a call for a male who had been injured while in line to get into a swap meet. This man had an older vehicle that had a problem with the drive shaft. The vehicle moved up the waiting line, and at one point a makeshift link pin fell out of the shaft. He knew immediately what the problem was, so he got out of the car and crawled under it to replace the pin.

The line of cars moved ahead, and the vehicle behind our soon-to-be patient honked its horn. Our patient's wife heard the honk and instinctively put the car in drive. The pin had been put back in place by this time, so the vehicle drove over the patients legs. This would have been bad enough by itself, but the *thump thump* of driving over our patient's legs made our patient's wife aware of what she had just done. To undo the damage, she threw the vehicle into reverse, only to hear the *thump, thump* again as she drove back over her husband a second time, breaking both his legs.

Be aware of your surroundings and who should be in the car.

CHIMNEY BOY

Santa Claus is said to be able to climb down chimneys and up them again by placing a finger alongside his nose, then giving a wink and a nod. Teenagers have a little more trouble with this, as it turns out.

I once responded to a young man, a latchkey kid who had lost his house key. No problem, just climb down the chimney, he thought. Some people learn the truth about this feat the hard way.

A very embarrassed and blackened young man was pulled up and returned to the ground.

Use a hide-a-key next time.

MR. LUCKY

Many people get divorced. It seems to be the norm rather than the exception. This couple managed to remain friends during and after the final separation. The ex-husband may not have been lucky in love but he was lucky not to receive a Darwin Award on this day.

Mr. D is a nice guy and helped Mrs. D in moving into her new home. He took in the boxes and settled the furniture. He even offered to hook up the washer and dryer.

Mr. D made all the appropriate connections to the dryer. To check the gas connection, he figured the best way to check would be to fire up his lighter. Guess what? He had a big leak. When we arrived, the laundry room fire had been put out with garden hoses, and his beard was a lot smaller and curlier.

Use soapy water to check for gas leaks, or hire a professional.

ZIPPER

People call the fire department when no other phone number seems to have an answer or specialization for a given problem. Whom do you call when your male appendage is caught in your zipper? This was not a child, but a full-grown man, who appeared to be in a great deal of pain. To humor the patient, the captain fired up a chain saw and said, "We'll get it out," and we did.

Do not be in a hurry when delicate parts are in use.

CLEANING WITH GAS

I responded to what had been an explosion and small fire in a second-floor apartment building. The fire was quickly put out, and we found out we had a patient in the courtyard pool. He was not hurt badly but was having trouble hearing.

It turns out this patient had been cleaning the walls with gasoline, filling the unit with vapors. The patient was from a third-world country and was not aware of wall furnaces and how they work. The wall furnace kicked on and flashed over, causing an explosion and hurling the patient into the pool below.

Do not use flammable liquids around ignition sources.

PANCAKE HAND

What is the quickest way to clean a roller-style printing press? This great idea came to the adult son of the business owner. He thought it would be quick and easy to clean the rollers while the machine was on. If you are thinking this couldn't have gone well, you are one step ahead of our eventual patient.

The machine grabbed his rag, then sucked his rag, fingers, hand and arm up through the rollers. We had to partially disassemble and then saw through portions of the case-hardened steel rollers to get his hand out. The hand resembled a pancake, as you would imagine it may look like in a cartoon.

I saw the young man months later when he came in to thank us for coming to his aid. All his fingers were saved except his thumb. His hand had been sewn to his upper leg to accommodate a skin graft. When the graft healed, the hand was once again freed, and he was thankful for the miracles of modern medicine!

A large toe was then removed from one of his feet and attached to his hand to replace the thumb. Unfortunately, the toe graft did not take.

Clean equipment in the manner recommended by the manufacturer.

CLEANING MAN

This is another cleaning accident. Late one night while a large manufacturing business was closed, the janitor was hard at work. The chore for this night was to clean the bathroom terrazzo floor.

The janitor thought that if he used Acetone and a buffer, the floor would clean up in no time at all. He spread the liquid all over the floor and plugged in the buffer. As soon as he pulled the trigger on his buffer, a spark from the motor set the entire floor on fire. It quickly engulfed him before the fire went out on its own.

The approaching fire engines were greeted by a ghostly figure walking toward the front gate like a zombie from *The Night of the Living Dead*. The janitor's clothing had burned away, and flesh seemed to be melting from his arms. He had second-degree burns over a large portion of his body.

Read product labeling, and do not use flammable liquids around sources of ignition, such as motors.

CHICKEN BREATH

Many rest-home nurses speak English as a second language. On one emergency call, I was met at the door and asked the nurse what the problem was.

"Chicken breath, chicken breath," was the answer.
"People don't die from chicken breath, slower please, what is the problem?"

"Chee .. con ... breth. Chee ... con ... breth."

When I reached the patient, it was clear that what the nurse was trying to say was, "She can't breath."

I was to go on many more "Chicken Breath" calls over the next 30 years.

Chapter 38

Fires/Investigations

HANDCUFFS

When I first started handling the fire investigation duties, I was partnered with a police detective. I was to learn police skills from him, and he was to learn fire-scene investigation from me. He had been conducting burglary investigations, and fire investigation was going to be one more additional task for him, just as police investigation would be an additional task for me.

My police counterpart was investigating a burglary in our community and was called to a neighboring city because they were holding a suspect for him. When my partner arrived at the neighboring city, he was told that they were not going to hold the suspect, and that my partner could take custody of the suspect. My partner was in an unmarked vehicle that did not have a rear seat cage, and he didn't have handcuffs with him.

No problem, an officer from the neighboring city said, "We'll just use flex-ties (plastic handcuffs) to hold him." The unmarked vehicle, having no cage in the back, meant the suspect had to ride up front, so that the suspect could be watched.

During the short trip back to our city jail, the suspect got loose from the ties and began wrestling for my partner's gun. They were at a signal light when the fight took place, it was clear that there was going to be only one winner, and I'm told my partner was on the short end. At that very moment, a highway patrol officer pulled up to the stoplight on his motorcycle. My partner, seeing the officer, yelled "shoot him, shoot him!"

The sounds of the shots thundered within the enclosed vehicle. The suspect lay dead in the front seat of the unmarked vehicle. My partner knew that if the CHP officer hadn't done what he did, he would have been dead himself. My partner had to take a few days off due to stress and ringing ears.

OIL REFINERY FIRE

It was the late 1970's, and I was working out of the headquarters station, assigned to the rescue unit. I had spoken to my wife by phone after she had learned that the oil refinery had a large explosion and fire. I assured her that I was on the rescue that day, that the truck had responded to the fire, and that I was staying in our city.

Our fire truck had been on scene for a few hours but returned back to quarters once the fire appeared to be under control. Once in quarters, the truck captain went home sick. I was told to slide over to the truck and fill in for the captain for the remainder of the shift, and someone was called in to back-fill my position.

In the meantime, back at the refinery fire, one of the remaining trucks had accidentally directed a straight stream of water into a tank of oil, disturbing the foam layer that had been laid down to smother the fire. This action caused the fire to erupt to a greater extent than it had originally been.

My truck was toned out to respond back to the fire. On scene, I walked past one of the workers who had been at the plant when it originally exploded. He was charred to a crisp, with his arms and legs frozen in a runners position, as if he had been burned while running and just fell to the ground in that position. I learned that a second worker had met the same fate as this worker.

The fire apparently was started by a gas leak. The workers knew it was a huge problem and started running. The gas cloud was ignited by a passing car, and the vehicle's passenger, a local police officer's daughter, also died in the ensuing explosion.

We sent the truck basket up, and I spent the rest of the night directing water onto the fire until relieved at the scene the next morning by the on-coming truck firefighters.

FIREWORKS

As the department's fire investigator, I guess I was viewed as a fire-cop and therefore also had to handle the duty of fireworks enforcement. Fireworks, in any form, were illegal and had been since 1930.

But fireworks were legal in a neighboring city, and our citizens would travel to that city for their fireworks. I would travel through the streets of our city during daylight hours and confiscate any fireworks I saw in use. However, as night fell, I would retreat for fear of causing a riot.

One year, I received a telephone call from an acquaintance working for the State Fire Marshals Office. They had been conducting surveillance of a large fireworks stand in Nevada. If they saw a vehicle with California plates purchase fireworks and then turn around and head back for the California border, the investigators would run the license plate. The investigators would then call investigators for the jurisdiction to which the suspects were headed. When I received my phone call, I contacted my partners at the police department. They were not impressed with this information and didn't want to pursue the lead, as if illegal fireworks were beneath them. I persisted, and the squeaky wheel got some action. I couldn't follow the lead myself because I was assigned to an engine company that day. I was given a lone detective who followed the lead to a business address.

When the suspect got to the location, a search of the vehicle and the business was conducted. What was found turned into a media event. It turned out to be the largest fireworks bust in the state that year. Over 500 pounds of illegal fireworks were recovered, along with several stolen telephone booth phones. The police department was happy to take credit for the bust and smiled for the cameras. I was just happy they listened to me.

I did have one interview with a noted newscaster in the Los Angeles Area. He introduced himself in what I thought was an odd manner. He said, "Hi, my name is Stan Chambers, do you know who I am?"

This man had been reporting the news since television was invented, and pretty much everyone in the greater L.A. area knew who Stan Chambers was. I have never been impressed with fame or position, so without thinking, I answered "Hi, my name is Mike Cunningham, do you know who I am?"

Looking back, it probably came across as impolite, but he struck me as a little pompous, and it had been a long day.

MOBILE HOME FIRES

City fire departments have stations that are fairly close together, making response time to fires pretty good. With a quick response time, firefighters can get to most fires fast enough to prevent a lot of damage to most dwelling type structures. Mobile homes, particularly the older ones, are not like most dwellings. The metal exteriors, thin, wood-covered walls, narrow halls and low ceilings make for very fast and very hot fires. Not many of these fires are fought from the interior. Mobile homes that catch fire in the middle of the night while the occupants are asleep usually result in deaths.

I was charged with conducting a scene investigation of one

such fire. Neighbors were interviewed, and they said that they could hear the cries of the occupants — an elderly male and his wife. The cries had stopped quickly, long before firefighters arrived.

The heaviest damage was at one end of the home near the living room, while the bedroom was the least damaged. The area of fire origin was traced back to a reclining chair. A full ashtray was still on the coffee table. It appeared that this may have been due to an unattended cigarette. One last cigarette before turning in for the night. The ash or butt falls between the cushion, and it can smolder for two or more hours before it breaks out in fire.

The bedroom was not heavily damaged by the fire, but the walls were heavily stained by smoke. I found the two victims on the floor, one on the left side of the bed and the second on the right side. What most probably occurred was that they were awoken by the sound of the fire and stood up at some point. The super heated, smoke-filled air filled their lungs and seared their throats closed. The victims likely dropped where they had stood and taken their last breath. I found the only charring in this room to be to the carpet around the mouth of the male victim. This marked his last exhale; where he expired the super-heated air.

If they had had a smoke detector, a second exit or had stayed low, where the air is cooler and less smoky, we might have seen a better outcome.

THE LOLLIPOP CAPER

Arson is very hard to prove, and in its early beginnings, the Arson Squad was fondly referred to as the "Catch and Release Team." It seemed, at first anyway, that we were only able to prosecute the dumb or criminally stupid. This was one such case where the perpetrators were not thinking. An alarm was toned out for a fire at a community pool. This was a building that had an office, a couple of restrooms and a pool in the rear yard. This property was used for private swimming lessons.

The fire broke out at night and was caught before it did a lot of damage. The firefighters found that the walls were covered with graffiti, and furniture had been tossed into the pool. The on-duty fire investigator had been keeping an eye on the growing crowd of spectators and noted that while most people were in their night clothing, two young men were on bikes and clothed. This seemed unusual for that time of night.

The investigators thought to interview them. They must have been awake and saw something ... or they may be suspects themselves. During the interviews, he noted that the young men were sucking on lollipops and that their pockets were bulging with candy. The young men were detained by police officers while an interview was conducted with the business owner.

The business owner stated that she did not have any enemies that she was aware of, and that she had closed up hours earlier. She said that every time a child leaves the swimming lesson, they are given a lollipop.

Firefighters stated that they found no lollipops on the premises, but the investigator remembered the suckers who were on their bikes. They later confessed to the crime.

THE WITNESS

I responded to a fire in an apartment complex as captain on the first arriving engine company. This was no ordinary apartment building, however. The complex housed medicated, mentally challenged people. The tenants were free to come and go as they pleased, and a 24-hour caretaker was on the premises to disburse medication. This caretaker also held the medical charts for each tenants.

On this night, the dispatcher got a call from someone who told her that his apartment was on fire and that he knew who started the fire. As the dispatcher toned out the various fire units, she also dispatched the police department. The caller was kept on the line and provided a detailed description of the alleged fire-starter.

The responding police officer got on scene to find the caller still on the pay phone: the caller had described himself, down to the shoes he was wearing.

The paranoid schizophrenic had set the fire himself, then called 911 to report the fire that his alter ego set.

This should have been an easy case, but it was not prosecutable. Children and the mentally disadvantaged cannot be found guilty of crimes. I have always had a problem with "not guilty by reasons of insanity or diminished capacity." What's wrong with *guilty* by reason of insanity or diminished capacity?

RECORDING STUDIO FIRES

I was called to a neighboring city to aid in the investigation of a very large fire. The two-story building had been owned by one member of a famous singing duo and was being used as a recording studio. I was not in charge of this investigation, so I don't know what the final determination was, but what follows are the circumstances as I know them.

The owner of the building had been Ike Turner. I was in charge of conducting several interviews. One such interview was of the owner's girlfriend, who looked an awful lot like a young Tina Turner.

The studio had been up for sale for some time. The studio had several offers on it but kept falling out of escrow.
At the time of the fire, a goodwill deposit had been made, and the property was back in escrow. It looked as if this young buyer was

going to qualify, and the deal was going to close at midnight. The horrible fire, involving flammable liquids, occurred before midnight. The beneficiary of the insurance would have been the original owner, not the young buyer.

Since this fire occurred in another jurisdiction, I don't know the final resolution of this fire or if a suspect was ever developed. However, I am aware that Ike Turner fell on hard times, and he went to jail years later on a drug-related crime.

The next studio fire I went on was as a private investigator. The fire originated in the middle of a large room which had hardwood floors and no obvious sources of ignition nearby. I noted a distinct pattern on the floor, indicative of something pooling and burning at floor level.

The story I got from interviews fit what I was seeing. The Black Eyed Peas musical group was in the studio for what turned out to be an all-night recording session. The studio was using the large room, where the fire started, to record an album. The room had several large foam rubber pillars used for controlling sound. Someone decided they wanted some mood lighting for the session, so a candle was brought in.

The band finished its session in the early-morning hours and was taking a break in a back room while a sound engineer finished mixing the tracks. The engineer noted heavy black smoke filling the adjacent room, where the band had just been. He alerted the band and other people in the building before rushing outside himself. The engineer then ran back inside the building and rescued the recordings of what eventually became the next Black Eyed Peas album.

The candle apparently had been knocked over, or perhaps it burned down and fell over, contacting the foam sound barriers. This foam produces large amounts of toxic, black smoke.

The foam also melts into burning pools of liquid. My recommendation to the insurance company was simply to not allow candles in rooms with those kinds of foam barriers.

A FISH TALE

As a fire investigator, my toughest investigation involved a wholesale business that was dealing in tropical fish.

The warehouse-style building was situated near Los Angeles International Airport. This was essential to the business because it had fish flown in from around the world. Once at LAX, the fish needed to be put back into tanks that replicated their natural environment quite quickly or they would die. This business would then sell fish to pet stores around the greater Los Angeles area.

The fire was obviously set in the office area using flammable liquids, and no signs of forced entry were found. I also noticed that the fire sprinkler system had been shut off, and the shut-off spanner was later found in a trash dumpster on the property. My thought was that the suspect had to have had a key and at least a passing knowledge of the sprinkler system.

The owner was interviewed first. Her actions and answers seemed evasive and rang as false to me. Finally, she admitted that she had been having an affair with a married man and that the two of them had been at a hotel at the time of the fire. The hotel registry and an interview with her partner seemed to confirm her story. Furthermore, the business seemed healthy, she appeared devastated by the fire, and was underinsured for the loss of the fish. She didn't seem to have a motive for arson.

I asked who had keys to the business and if she had any enemies. She had only a couple of employees, but one was of particular interest; he had just been fired. This employee had been essential in setting up fish tanks with the right temperatures and salinity levels for the fish. Further inquiries about this employee revealed he had been a firefighter at one time. So he not only had a motive, but he also had special knowledge about fire sprinkler systems.

It eventually came out that this employee had imagined that he and the business owner were a couple and that he was a principal partner in the business. The owner assured me that neither were true. What got the employee fired was that he began stalking the owner and had been detained by sheriff's deputies after being found in her backyard wielding a machete. A restraining order and notice of his firing followed.

I started doing research on this new suspect. I went to the fire department where he had worked and learned that he had been dismissed for pulling an automatic weapon on his supervisor. It was easy to conclude that my suspect may be deranged, delusional and dangerous.

The fire investigator of this other department told me my suspect once asked him, "How would you set a fire and not get caught?"

I was able to get a search warrant for the suspect's phone records and learned that he had called someone in Las Vegas several times just prior to the fire. This someone, it turned out, was a security guard for the MGM Grand and a former firefighter himself, who had retired due to a bad back.

I traveled to Las Vegas (a tough job, but someone had to do it) to question the guard about our suspect. I also asked the guard where he had been at the time of the fire. He said the phone calls were about a request that he come to Los Angeles to help the suspect and another person move a large fish tank upstairs. When asked how he could have done that with his bad back, he pleaded his Fifth Amendment rights and ended the interview.

Next I interviewed the third man in this fish-tank moving caper. He and his estranged wife were having financial problems and filed for bankruptcy. It seemed he had a very expensive drug habit that interfered with the marriage.

I eventually found a restaurant with employees who remembered seeing these three "fish-tank movers" dining together in a city near Los Angeles shortly before the fire occurred. So now I had motive and opportunity for all three suspects. I went to a judge with my story and my reports. He issued an arrest warrant for the employee, my primary suspect. The suspect wouldn't talk, evoking his Fifth Amendment rights.

I took my evidence to the District Attorney's office in order to get a filing on the case. The D.A. apparently didn't think the case was as strong as I did, and he apparently didn't know that circumstantial evidence was acceptable in arson cases. The D.A. asked me to follow the suspect with the drug problem and catch him with drugs, then offer him immunity in exchange for his testimony in the arson case.
I thought, "I'm a firefighter, my chief will never go for me getting involved in drug busts."

I was right. In fact, my chief was not too wild about me getting involved in any portion of fire investigation beyond the fire scene itself. So apparently a violent suspect goes free as part of the "Catch and Release Team."

Later, an "unknown person" climbed to the roof of the fish warehouse, pulled open a vent, and poured diesel fuel into the fish tanks below, killing all the fish once again. I just have to wonder who might have done such a thing. I contacted the Bureau of Alcohol, Tobacco and Firearms about my problem child, and they were able to put a 24-hour surveillance camera on the fish business. Unfortunately, or perhaps fortunately, no further crimes were committed at that location.

DEAD MEN TELL NO TALES

You may remember this story because parts of it were incorporated into the fictionalized story at the beginning of this book.

A warehouse fire in one particular part of the city was not that unusual, but this one had a dead man in the middle of the building. I was called in from home to conduct the investigation. The first arriving captain thought that a large warehouse fire after midnight with a dead person was noteworthy enough.

I quickly learned that the fire had involved flammable liquids and that it had multiple areas of origin. I thought finding the suspect was going to be easy; after all, a dead man was on the floor. Maybe the fire got away from him. Maybe he became disoriented and died in the smoke. It turned out that having dead people in this warehouse was not all that unusual. In fact, it was quite normal. The building stored dead people for a company that turns bodies into ash for later disposal at sea. However, the bodies were supposed to be in a large, walk-in refrigerator, not on the floor.

I turned over the body and saw that his shirt was open. He had three electrode patches on his chest, the type of electrodes that paramedics use on patients who have chest pain. This body was a customer, not a suspect.

I interviewed the owner by phone. He said he was in Las Vegas. It's amazing how many people are in Vegas at the time of a fire in their business. Bad luck, I guess. I asked him to meet with me when he was in town.

Then I interviewed an employee and asked when he was last in the building. He explained that when a customer is picked up, the body is brought to the warehouse, and a card would be made with the deceased's name on it. The card is run through the punch clock, and the customer stored in the cooler. The employee said he punched in a customer a little after midnight on the night of the fire and found nothing wrong in the warehouse at that time.

He then left, but added that the owner was still in the building at that time. This owner had previously told me that he was in Vegas at the time of the fire. I could not eliminate him as a suspect, but what is the motive?

I found out that the owner/suspect was the son of a man who had shot and killed a gang member during a robbery attempt. The owner/suspect would later blame the fire on gang members. I also found out that my owner/suspect had numerous insurance claims over the years. This was not criminal, but it certainly seemed like a sign that he was unluckier than most. I also could not eliminate gang members as suspects.

While I was still at the fire scene, an unmarked white van pulled up, and two men began tossing "customers" into the back of the van like so much cord wood.

A repairman from Southern California Edison walked in at that time to work on the electrical system, saw what was happening with the bodies, and quickly retreated outside the building to vomit. He never returned to the building while I was still there.

Eventually, I was able to conduct a face-to-face interview with the owner and confronted him about his Las Vegas story. He quickly changed his story, saying he was confused about the day of the fire.

I wasn't able to get a filing on this loss, but I did receive a call from an informant. The tipster told me that the owner had been smuggling in drugs from Arizona. He would place packets of drugs into a cavity cut into a customer's shoulder. This packet would look like it was a pacemaker, and who would suspect drugs in a dead body? My informant also stated the owner would run hookers over to mortuaries as a courtesy to morticians, who sent work his way.

It turned out that my informant was a felon, so the DA deemed him "not to be a credible source" and didn't want to put him before a jury. I would have liked to believe him, but we could not corroborate his story. This informant was already in jail for another crime and I'm not sure what he had to gain by lying.

A SPRAY OF FIRE

During my time with the fire department, I spent many years as a private investigator working for various insurance companies. Insurance companies hire private investigators because fire department reports are short and vague. Many departments have gone to computerized reports that print out phrases based on a number placed in a check box. This abbreviated report may indicate a fire was in a "bedroom or sleeping quarters/other," and the cause as being "electrical."

Insurance companies can't rely on this type of reporting. The insurance companies need precise locations and descriptions with photographs. If the fire was electrical, was it due to a fault in the building, some product belonging to the tenant, or an act on the part of the tenant, owner or insured?

This information can tell the insurance company who is responsible: the tenant or the owner/insured. If a product caused the fire, was it faulty, and can restitution be recovered from some third party?

On this call, a very nice home belonging to an Iranian couple caught fire in the middle of the night during a major remodel. The home was occupied at the time, but the insured and his family escaped uninjured.

The fire burned from under the raised foundation and extended up and into a newly remodeled kitchen. The electrical components running under the dwelling were burned, but no obvious signs of an electrical failure were found. A gas meter had been under the dwelling, but it had been removed from the scene by the gas company prior to my investigation.

I suppose a gas leak may have formed, but what was the heat source, and why was there no explosion if a leak had occurred?
While under the house, I dug up the soft earth around where the gas meter had been, just out of curiosity.

I retreated from under the dwelling and took a whiff of the earth that filled the bottom of my container. It was gasoline, no mistake about it. Gasoline had not been stored there, so how did it get there?

The owner/insured stated he had no known enemies and that his children were too young to have developed any. I suggested to the insured that he invest in surveillance cameras to protect himself. My report listed the cause as incendiary; that is, fire that was intentionally set by a human. I could not tell who set the fire, but I told the insurance company that I did not suspect the owner/insured. This allows an insurance company to pay off the loss even if the fire department and I can't determine who set the fire.

A couple of months went by, and the same owner/insured had a second fire, started in the same exact place and fashion. This time, because the owner followed my advice to install surveillance camera, it was caught on video from six different angles.

A straight stream of a liquid could be seen coming from over the fence from a neighboring property and toward the crawl space, where the gas meter had been. Moments later a flare, attached to a long stick, was seen coming over the fence, igniting the gasoline. The stick with the flare was then pulled back over the fence, and the fire continued to burn the insured's dwelling.

Police officers were shown the videos moments after the fire was extinguished. The officers went to the neighboring yard to find the dirt planter had been freshly raked. A search warrant was obtained and the property searched.

A detective retrieved a stick with a flare attached to it, and in the suspect's vehicle was a Hudson sprayer that had been modified to spray a straight stream. The sprayer still had gasoline in it. The suspect was then charged with two counts of arson and four counts of attempted murder.

MY MOMMY SAID I DIDN'T DO IT

The three leading causes of fire are men, women and children. If a fire starts in a closet of a child's room, you can bet that a child was unsupervised, and that someone in the home smokes. This was the case of one such closet fire that destroyed a child's bedroom and blackened the rest of the house.

It's one thing to have a child lie about an event such as starting a fire, but when I spoke with the child, he said, "My mommy said I did not do it."

I questioned the boy's mother, who also said that her son could not have caused the fire. She said this between drags on her cigarette. If a parent doesn't know right from wrong, how does one expect the child to know right from wrong?

This child was much too young to have done anything criminal, in a legal sense, so nothing would have happened to the boy. However, I wanted to know if I had a curious child or a problem fire-setter on my hands. Despite what Mommy said, my report read that the child set the fire. It was either that or mice with matches, and most mice know better.

This would normally be the end of the story, but sadly, it is not. I used to counsel children and parents to determine if a child had a problem, or if it was just a case of curiosity. Every child fire-setter I came upon was a male between 4 and 7 years of age. This is the age of curiosity. A child who has a fire problem, in every case I worked, came from a single-parent home, and the child had been sexually abused. Every one!

These children feel helpless and without power. They act out by being cruel to animals and destructive to personal belongings, long before they set things on fire. The child fire-setter will grow up to be an adolescent fire-setter, and later an adult fire-setter. The fires getting bigger with each start.

In interviewing neighbors, I learned that my fire-setter had been kicking neighborhood cats and breaking toys against a tree.

I again spoke with Mommy and told her of the seriousness of the problem if not treated soon.

I asked the mother point-blank if the child had been molested. Her eyes widened, and she said, "Yes." She gave me the name of the individual who had molested her son. I bowed my head in frustration, as the name I heard was someone who, as a youngster years earlier, was arrested for setting fire to a grocery store. I was the one who arrested him.

The circle continues, the abused set fires, and then they abuse children themselves. The newly abused beat kittens and set new fires. An arsonist is born, and the circle continues because "Mommy said I did not do it."

KIDS WITH LIGHTERS

Early in my fire investigation career, I learned of a fire that a 6-year-old had started in his bedroom with a lighter. The child lived in an apartment house with his mother. The child apparently crossed a busy street, walked into a grocery store and bought a lighter. We have laws about what age you have to be to buy cigarettes, but at that time, we had no such laws on what age you have to be to buy a lighter. I would like to think that a grocery clerk would not sell lighters to children, but that's not the case.

When the child's mother was told of the sequence of events that led to the fire, she was most upset that he crossed the street without permission. She did not seem as upset that he had just burned out her dwelling and those of several neighbors.

I worked another fire near Los Angeles International Airport for an insurance company. The fire occurred in a condominium that was part of a gated community. Two children died in the fire, and I had to conduct the scene investigation.

The fire reached every room of the two-story, two-bedroom condo. I was able to trace the area of origin back to the living room, where a sofa bed had been located. A young girl died in a closet of one of the bedrooms, while a small boy had died near the closet of the second bedroom.

The condominium was owned by the children's grandmother, who was their guardian. The children's mother was in jail for reasons unknown to me. It was later learned that the young boy was playing with a lighter, his sister was playing elsewhere, and grandma was cooking dinner. Grandma saw a small fire in the sofa but did not call 911 right away. Instead, she tried to put the fire out with a pan of water. Grandma finally figured that she couldn't put the fire out after a couple of attempts with pans of water.

The fire got out of control, so Grandma ran from the building. She told me that she thought she had ushered out the children while calling out to neighbors to call 911. Apparently unknown to Grandma, her granddaughter was still upstairs. While Grandma was calling for help, her grandson ran back into the dwelling to get his sister.

Grandma was asked why she didn't get out right away and have neighbors call 911. She reported that her grandson had caused other fires, and she was afraid that he would be taken away if it was learned that he started another fire. Another problem fire-setter, and a product of a broken, single-parent home.

Months after this investigation, I learned that the grandmother and the biological father were suing the homeowners association over the deaths. The father had no apparent interest in the children until their deaths, and mom had since died in jail.

The lawsuit was over speed bumps in the community and a locked gate. It seems ironic that they put speed bumps in to save children from speeding cars, and now they were being blamed for slowing down a fire engine.

The attorneys questioned firefighters on why they didn't ram a gate with their fire engines. I knew the engineer driving the first-in fire engine, and he was fully aware of the proper gate to enter, and we don't ram gates with fire engines.

During preparation for the case, a team of fire modeling/computer experts were brought in. They plugged in room measurements, furnishings and wall coverings, along with heat-and-time temperature curves. The computer ran the figures for the better part of a day and came out with a video of the fire's progression. This fire model was compared to dispatch times and response times.

It concluded that the children died before dispatch toned out the first engine.

A CHILLY DAY

This fire involved a teenaged boy, and the fire was accidental. Mom and Dad were both teachers and were at their respective schools. Their teenaged son stayed home sick on that day.

I entered the scene as a private investigator, another insurance job. What I found was quite disturbing, since I had no one to interview at the time.

I found several areas of fire origin. One area had been in the living room, one in the kitchen, and another in the garage. I preferred to conduct my scene investigations prior to doing any interviews. This precluded me from being led or misled on areas of origin or cause.

After I conducted my interviews, the scene suddenly made sense. This was a tragic sequence of events that totally destroyed this family's home.

The weather was chilly for Southern California, so the teen tried to light the fireplace. He turned on the gas and lit the fire. He soon realized that the flue was closed. Before he could open the flue, a decorative mantle piece caught fire. The young man grabbed the burning pieces and tossed them into the kitchen sink, catching the kitchen drapes on fire. He looked back to see dried flowers on the hearth now burning. He grabbed the flowers and ran to the garage, where the garage began burning.

The teen opened the sliding glass door and ran to the rear yard to get a garden hose, but the hose was too short. He ran back inside the dwelling, leaving the sliding door open. He then ran upstairs and opened windows to yell out to neighbors. By then, a firestorm was created by leaving the first floor door open and the second floor windows open to vent the fire upstairs. First arriving firefighters had to remove the young man from the roof of the well-involved dwelling.

I WISH YOU WORKED FOR ME

I was sent to a garage fire as a private investigator. It was a detached garage on a residential property. The garage had been gutted, and it was full with quite a lot of furnishings at the time.

I met the insured, who allowed me access to the garage. Unsolicited, the insured told me that the fire department informed her that it had been a faulty garage door opener that caused the fire. I found the fire damage was much too heavy at floor level to have started in the area of the garage door opener. I eventually found charring on the bottom side of furnishings and a baby grand piano. These findings suggested a fire that burned at floor level.

I noted a lawn mower, but other than that, no quantities of flammable liquid that would account for floor-level burning. I drew my diagram, took photos and finished my interviews.

I next contacted the insurance company to let them know that I suspected that the fire had been set, and that the insured had to be considered among the suspects. I was told to go back and collect the garage door opener as evidence that it did not cause the fire.

I made my appointment with the insured again and returned to the scene. A friend of the insured was standing with the insured as I conducted this second scene investigation. The friend asked who I was. I answered.

"I'm a fire investigator, working for Ms. ..."
The insured, being on to me, being on to her, said, "Oh, I wish you worked for me!"

I quickly gathered up the portions of the garage door opener, and at the last moment I took samples of debris at floor level, hoping to find trace levels of the flammable liquid before the eagle-eyed insured ran me off.

I was returning home with the evidence when I received a call from my partner. He said that the insured just called and was very upset, and she wanted her stuff back. "What stuff, you mean the burned-up garage opener and the floor debris?"

I was thinking the insured was a little nervous, and something was definitely up. I phoned the local fire department investigator who had handled this loss and asked him if he had blamed the fire on the garage door opener. He said no, he listed the cause as undetermined, but he thought that it may have been set.

I finished my report and sent it on to the insurance company to let them decide whether to pay the loss or not. Several months went by, and I heard nothing more on the case until an L.A. City investigator called to inform me that I was set to testify before a Grand Jury Hearing.

It turned out that the insured had quite a business going, and insurance companies were unwitting partners. The insured was sticking furniture in a garage, setting it on fire and collecting insurance on supposed antiques. She would then move the charred furniture to a new location and set it on fire again, collecting insurance money again. She did this five or six times before she was caught and finally put on trial.

THE "CLEANING" JOB

I was sent to Los Angeles to conduct an investigation of a bar/dance club fire for an insurance company. The building was a two-story structure built into a hillside. The lower street level had an entrance. The driveway led up a hill to a parking lot and a second entrance.

I found obvious evidence of arson with flammable liquid trails upstairs and going down the stairs toward the lower level. During my interview with the L.A. City fire investigator, I learned a male was found dead on the lower level near the door.

When the wife of the deceased was interviewed, she said her husband had left late at night, saying that he had a "cleaning job." Not being a criminal investigator on this fire, my job was done once my report went to the insurance company.

What appeared to have happened is that the deceased entered the second floor and spread flammable liquid throughout the second floor and leading down to the first floor. He then lit the fire with the intention of exiting the first-floor door. Unfortunately, the first floor door was locked from the exterior.

If I could impart one final message to the reader, it is that life is not a destination or some goal that you're chasing. Those aspirations are constantly changing, either by design or due to circumstances beyond your control. The best you can do is put down solid building blocks and move on to the next block. If a building block is damaged due to mistakes or not to your liking because of circumstances, you — and only you — have the power to change it. Remember the adage that life is what happens while you're busy making other plans. Don't let it pass you by. Most importantly, family is the glue that holds together those building blocks. Love your family and enjoy yourself. Be kind to yourself and to your fellow man. Live your life not in fear of something tragic, but instead with a subtle sense of urgency. Humans are fragile, and life is short.